LOVE WILL FIND A WAY

Texan Darcy Benton would give anything to be the kind of woman who could captivate her new boss Chase Whitaker. However, the sexy CEO would hardly fall for someone like Darcy, with her straight-laced office wardrobe. Enter Darcy's match-making pal, Janet. She transforms her into a bombshell worthy of Chase's undying devotion. Darcy is soon letting her hair down and swapping her boxy suits for slinky dresses. And as Chase becomes intrigued — he's ready for anything . . . including true love.

JOAN REEVES

LOVE WILL FIND A WAY

Complete and Unabridged

LINFORD
Leicester

First published in
the United States of America in 1999

First Linford Edition
published 2008

British Library CIP Data

Reeves, Joan
  Love will find a way.—Large print ed.—
  Linford romance library
  1. Love stories
  2. Large type books
  I. Title
  813.5'4 [F]

  ISBN 978–1–84782–415–8

Published by
F. A. Thorpe (Publishing)
Anstey, Leicestershire

Set by Words & Graphics Ltd.
Anstey, Leicestershire
Printed and bound in Great Britain by
T. J. International Ltd., Padstow, Cornwall

This book is printed on acid-free paper

The greatest gifts are not always wrapped in shiny paper and tied with red bows. They sometimes come packaged as mothers. I've been blessed with three such wonderful gifts — women who've made my life immeasurably richer. I am who I am as a result of having them in my life.

This book is dedicated with appreciation, admiration, and love to my mother, Lucille Dickinson Ainsworth, my original mother-in-law, Helen Sims Lofton, and my present mother-in-law, Frances Smith Reeves.

And, as always, for L.A.R. Thanks for the memories!

1

Darcy Benton wondered if she needed to check into a hospital.

Her nervous system seemed to have shorted out, producing feet that felt like blocks of ice and hands that perspired as if it were July rather than December. Her heart was racing, and her face was fiery hot.

Releasing her white-knuckled grip on the strap of her new leather handbag, Darcy opened it and fished out one of the tissues she'd stashed inside.

Hoping that the man who'd created this shock to her system was still engrossed in reading her résumé, she furtively wiped her palms. For good measure, she blotted her damp forehead.

Her eyes strayed to the man on the power side of the mahogany desk. Chase Whitaker was the owner of

Sunbelt Oil Producers, one of the many small independent energy companies in San Antonio. His attention remained fixed on the paper he held.

Chase — she tried the name out in her mind. She liked it. It was unusual and suited him perfectly.

Feeling hot and cold by turns, Darcy examined his features as intently as he studied her résumé. His face easily rivaled any male heartthrob on the silver screen. His dark blue eyes could only be characterized as bedroom eyes. The phrase made Darcy tingle.

His thick ebony hair made her yearn to slide her fingers through the silky black strands. Just thinking about it made her sigh. And his mouth! Oh, my goodness! Darcy couldn't even put words to the feelings incited by his full, chiseled lips. Another sigh escaped her. At the soft sound, Chase shifted. His eyes flickered to her, then back to her résumé.

Darcy felt a blush begin beneath her prim white blouse and creep upwards until it reached her face. This would never do. She blotted her forehead again, surprised at how damp the tissue felt.

Frowning, she looked at it. Her eyes widened in shock. Blue ink practically dripped from the sodden wad of tissue. Horrified, she stared dumbly at the blue ink that colored her fingertips and rimmed her unpainted nails.

If any of her three brothers had been in the room, she'd have accused them of playing another of their dumb practical jokes. But this time, she only had herself — and a cheap ballpoint pen that had leaked over the contents of her expensive new purse — to blame for her fall from sophisticated femininity. Somehow, she thought in despair, she always ended up feeling and looking like the gangly kid who'd tried to outdo her older siblings in every sport.

Resigned, Darcy opened both palms. Blue ink — in-delible blue at that — mottled her pale skin. She looked at the shiny brass and glass table next to

3

her chair, with the ridiculous hope that there would be a box of tissues beneath the small Christmas tree decorated with tiny gold oil wells. No such luck. Desperate, she wiped her palms up and down the sides of her navy skirt.

With a prayer on her lips, Darcy looked at her hands again. The mottling had been replaced by wide smeary streaks. Great! Just great! It was no use. The ink wasn't going anywhere. She closed her hands into tight fists, trying to hide the stains.

Why had this happened when she wanted so desperately to make an impression on Chase Whitaker? And not just because she wanted him to hire her. The man stirred something inside her that she'd never felt in all her twenty-four years. Just looking at his hands made her quiver like a taut wire on a piano.

Her music teacher mother would describe his large, well-formed hands with long, shapely fingers, as pianist hands. Bronzed by the sun, his hands

4

contrasted sharply with the immaculate French cuffs of his starched white shirt. The thing Darcy liked most about his hands was the absence of a wedding ring on the left one.

That brought her up short. Get a grip, Darcy Benton, she scolded herself. You're here for a job — not a romantic entanglement. As if she would even know how to have a romantic entanglement, she thought sourly, determined to stifle her overactive imagination. But her fantasies refused to be silenced.

She prayed silently that she would get this accounting position. And not just because she had to start repaying her student loans. Darcy realized that she wanted this job more than she wanted air to breathe!

Another sigh escaped her. Chase glanced up, his eyes sharp and penetrating. He frowned. Surely he couldn't know what she'd been thinking. She felt her blush intensify. She watched him slowly wipe his hand across his forehead. His hand — and those bedroom eyes — mesmerized Darcy. Her breath seemed too expansive for her lungs.

Feeling light-headed, she uncrossed her legs, knocking over her briefcase. 'Sorry,' she mumbled. Her eyes rolled to the ceiling in disgust. Could she possibly appear more clumsy?

Then she realized that he seemed to look, not at her eyes, but about an inch above them. His irresistible mouth twitched as if a smile struggled to break free of restraint. He stood, and Darcy's mouth went dry as her gaze climbed his tall, broad-shouldered frame.

When she'd first entered his office, she'd had the unusual pleasure of looking up to meet his eyes, rather than down, as she usually did. She felt absurdly pleased that he was a few inches taller than her five feet eleven inches.

He reached into his back pocket and pulled out a snowy white square of linen and walked around the desk and offered it to her. 'This should help.'

Taken aback, she frowned. He touched his forehead again, making a wiping motion. Suddenly, horrified understanding flooded her. Quickly, she swiped the handkerchief across her forehead and wasn't surprised to see it come away streaked in blue. She didn't even want to think about what her forehead must look like.

She returned his handkerchief. Chase carefully folded it and laid it on his desktop. He remained standing, towering over her. She wished he would go back to his chair.

'Thank you, Mr. Whitaker,' she said, acting as if nothing were wrong. Her voice was brisk and cool. She was afraid to let any warmth creep into her voice for fear she'd cry, or worse, that he'd discover how breathless his nearness made her.

Each time she looked at him, she felt so peculiar, like the time her three brothers had dared her to climb the giant pine tree in the backyard and she'd fallen, knocking the breath out of her.

Belatedly, she realized that he was talking. She focused hard and caught the end of his sentence. ' — give you a chance. We'd wanted someone with experience, but we're willing to take you on, though we try not to hire straight out of college. But your class standing was excellent. And you seem like a mature, sober young woman.'

His eyes swept her up and down, from the tight knot of hair forced into submission by half a tube of gel, to the black, square-framed glasses. Those sexy eyes of his quickly took in her severe navy suit, pristine white blouse, and floppy navy bow tie.

The book she'd read on dressing for success had said this was the outfit professional women wore. She'd plunked down her credit card hoping that the book was right and the severe clothing would change her image from a basketball-playing tomboy to a stunning corporate diva. Maybe she should have checked the copyright date in the book, she thought, feeling uncertain.

His sexy eyes reached her size ten feet clad in sensible, low-heeled shoes — ugly black patent leather pumps that Darcy knew no fashionable woman her age would be caught dead wearing. But she'd thought they'd be perfect in case the owner of Sunbelt Oil turned out to be on the short side.

Chase cleared his throat. 'And you are obviously sensible and practical.' He smiled.

Mature? Sober? Sensible? Practical?

Why didn't he just say she was so undesirable that even a man ship-wrecked on a desert island for twenty years wouldn't put the moves on her? Darcy fumed, insulted by his assessment.

The rest of what he said faded into the distance. Just once, why couldn't she be seen as incredibly sexy or completely irresistible! Why couldn't he be as attracted to her as she was to him?

When he offered her the accounting position for which she had applied, Darcy coolly thanked him. She knew she was being ridiculous, acting like a starry-eyed teenager in the throes of infatuation, but she couldn't help it. She hadn't had enough experience with infatuation to become blasé about it.

She tried to work up some satisfaction at landing her first real job, but she felt more depressed than elated. Well, she might as well get over it, she told herself. Even had she managed to attract Chase's attention, she'd never have stood a chance.

Even with her limited experience with the opposite sex, Darcy recognized the kind of man he was — a real heartbreaker. It was stamped on him as indelibly as the ink that stained her fingers. He was completely out of her league — from his bedroom eyes to his delectable mouth.

'Welcome to Sunbelt Oil,' he said, offering his hand to her. Pulse pounding, Darcy stood and stepped toward him. She'd forgotten about her briefcase, but it hadn't forgotten about her, she thought as she stumbled over it.

Momentum pitched her toward Chase. He reached up and grabbed her hands, catching her before she did a half-gainer and landed face first at his feet.

Smoothly, his grip changed to a handshake. Laughter danced in his sexy eyes. 'Again, welcome to Sunbelt,' he said smoothly.

'Thank you, Mr. Whitaker.' His touch was everything she had imagined it would be — more's the pity. His skin warmed her suddenly icy hand. The touch of his palm to hers was flame to dry tinder. Suddenly, Darcy fully understood the definition of the word *desire*. Her pulse throbbed in places she hadn't suspected could throb.

Mortified by her discovery, she jerked her hand back. She'd die if he ever knew how she felt! Determined that he never know how he affected her, she thanked him in a brisk, cool voice. She might as well squelch her hopeless romantic notions, Darcy told herself, because she knew that Chase Whitaker saw nothing, absolutely nothing, that attracted him.

Why couldn't she be petite, cute, and sexy — with a flair for fashion rather than a killer hoop shot? Why did she have to be a tomboy who towered over nearly every man in the state of Texas?

Darcy managed a few strangled words conveying her pleasure at joining his company even as a horrible suspicion began forming in her mind. She rejected the idea — it was unthinkable! Perfectly ridiculous, in fact!

When Chase touched her elbow, Darcy knew she was a goner. He led her to the door, which was a good thing, because the way her head was spinning, she'd never have found it on her own.

Somehow, she found her way back to her little blue car in the parking lot. Huddled on the cold vinyl seat, she stared at the office building and wondered which window was his.

'What am I going to do?' Darcy moaned.

Working near Chase Whitaker, who

had looked at her as if she were another piece of office furniture that he'd just acquired, was going to be impossible.

Crazy as it was, Darcy realized that she had fallen in love at first sight with her handsome new boss.

2

'Darcy,' Janet Wu whispered from her perch on the edge of Darcy's desk. 'Why don't you ask Chase to the Christmas party?'

Darcy ignored her best friend, who seemed to want nothing more than to irritate her today.

'I can't hear you. I can't hear you,' she sang to the tune of *Jingle Bells*, which she'd been humming softly when Janet had plopped her leather-clad fanny on top of the drilling expense reports on Darcy's desk.

'Well, if you'd quit humming those Christmas carols, maybe you could!' Janet said.

Darcy smiled complacently and continued stacking the copies of the year-end financial statements, whacking the end of each pile against her desktop — partially to maintain the straightness of each stack, but mostly to drown out Janet's comments. Apparently, Janet had decided not to take no for an answer when she'd first broached the matter yesterday over Sunday brunch.

'I swear,' Janet grumbled. 'For two years you've had the hots for that man. It's time you did something about it.'

Like what? Darcy didn't say. Her eyes sought the man who was the subject of their conversation.

Chase Whitaker stood in the doorway beneath a sprig of fake mistletoe. Her eyes devoured him. He'd been in New York for two weeks, and she had missed him dreadfully.

'Just walk over to him and plant one on him,' Janet urged.

The financial reports catapulted out of Darcy's hands in a white blizzard and landed all over the beige carpet in front of her cubicle.

'Janet! See what you made me do?' Darcy kneeled to retrieve the papers, thankful of the opportunity to hide her crimson face. Janet didn't know the meaning of subtle, she thought grumpily, staring at her friend's pretty face, now crinkled in a huge grin.

The day Janet had accused her of being in love with Chase, Darcy wished she had denied it until the cows came home.

Instead, she'd confessed her foolish secret. And found out that Janet had known Chase since their fathers, best friends who'd served together in the Air Force, had plunked them down in the same sandbox. She seemed determined to throw Darcy at Chase.

Unfortunately, as the months had passed, her friend was getting less and less subtle in her suggestions, too.

'I would help you, but these leather trousers don't bend so well at the knee,' Janet said.

'Maybe if you got a bigger size, they might,' Darcy sniped, gathering up pages.

Janet chuckled. 'You're probably right, but they wouldn't look as good, now would they?'

Darcy laughed in spite of herself. 'Yeah, I have to admit, Janet, you look like God's gift to mankind in that leather outfit.' Her best friend's petite figure, almond eyes, and sleek black hair were almost unfair. 'I'm sure you won't have any trouble finding someone to help you recover from the broken heart you were telling me about yesterday.'

'Already have!' Janet said smugly. 'Kevin G. O'Donnell is his name — and the G is for totally gorgeous! But don't change the subject. We were talking about you, and your date for the Christmas party. I think you ought to ask Chase. I know for a fact that he doesn't have a date.'

The financial reports went flying again. Darcy groaned. 'Just be quiet, would you?'

Janet snickered. 'I remember when you first came to work here. It seemed as if you dropped everything you touched. Then I noticed that it was only when Chase was around. Just seeing him turned you into Super Klutz.'

'Please keep your comments to yourself. If you're not going to help, just go back to your desk,' Darcy snapped.

'Now, now, don't be nasty.'

'At least keep your voice down,' Darcy said, looking around to make sure her coworkers were engrossed in the business of running Sunbelt Oil. She would have said more, but her mouth seemed to go on strike suddenly. Chase was coming toward them.

'Can I help?' he asked kindly, kneeling next to Darcy.

Her breath caught, trapping the masculine scent of his aftershave in her lungs.

'Hey, Chase! How ya doin'?' Janet asked, grinning. 'We were just talking about you.'

Darcy's eyes rounded in horror. Surely Janet wouldn't — ?

'Oh, really?' Chase asked absently. Darcy noted his powerful thighs flexing beneath charcoal wool trousers as he reached to pick up a stray page. Then he handed the pile he'd gathered to Darcy. She felt as if she had mittens on her hands. Clumsily, she gathered the mass to her, wrinkling the crisp pages.

'We were just talking about the Christmas party Friday night. We're really looking forward to it. Should be great fun if the last two were any standard to go by.'

Darcy wanted to kick her best friend — or have her fitted for a muzzle. Instead, she contented herself with standing and towering over her talkative buddy. She glared at Janet, hoping she'd develop a sudden capacity for discretion.

Janet caught her eye and winked. Darcy was certain that the spinning planet lurched for a microsecond. She willed her friend not to say anything else, but it was no use.

'Yeah, Darcy and I wondered who you were taking to the party?'

Darcy shuddered and contemplated murder. Maybe she could stash Janet's mischievous body inside one of the file cabinets later?

Chase laughed. 'I hadn't decided, unless you're asking me. Want to make it a friendly date?'

Janet laughed and punched him in the bicep. 'No way! Think I'd get all dolled up for a guy I can't make out with?'

'Then I guess I'm safe.' Chase chuckled.

Darcy listened to their good-natured banter and wished she possessed a fraction of that nonchalance. Wistfully, she looked at them, laughing and joking. Why couldn't she ignore the unrequited love that plagued her and just act like Janet? But her whole body coiled into a tight spring whenever Chase approached. She could hardly breathe, much less think rationally.

With a doleful sigh, she crushed the pile of papers to her chest and sank onto her chair. At least she didn't have these stupid accidents quite so often anymore, she thought, knowing she'd have to reprint the stack of financial reports.

'What about you?' Chase asked.

Darcy's head jerked up. 'What about me?'

Dismayed, she stared as if he'd asked her to recite the periodic table of elements.

'Who are you going to the party with?' he asked.

She hadn't attended the other two Christmas parties and had no plans to make an exception this year. But a shred of feminine pride reared its head. She couldn't stand for him to know that she didn't have a date. But she couldn't lie either. She opted for what she hoped looked like an eloquent shrug. He could read anything into that he wished. From the corner of her eye, she saw Janet shake her head in disgust.

'Oh, Darcy hasn't decided yet either,' Janet said suddenly. Her lips pursed, thoughtfully, and her almond eyes narrowed as she looked from Darcy to Chase.

'Well, you'd better make up your mind. Today's Monday,' Chase reminded. He stretched and rocked back on his heels.

Darcy saw Janet's eyes widen. She didn't like that look on her friend's face. It didn't bode well for her, she knew.

Janet said airily, 'Oh, Darcy always has so many men after her that she has a tough time choosing.'

It was all Darcy could do not to drop the disordered pile of papers again. Aghast, she stared at Janet. What on earth was the woman doing?

'Oh, really?' Chase asked. He looked over at Darcy as if expecting to see someone different. Then he grinned and said, 'Well, hurry up, Darcy, and make some poor guy happy.'

Darcy couldn't even look at him, much less reply to his teasing statement. If Chase would just leave immediately and return to his office, she'd only kill Janet a little bit, she bargained silently.

She risked a glance at Chase and her face flamed. The lines around the corners of his eyes crinkled. He seemed to be fighting a battle to hold in his laughter. With his next words, she wanted to crawl beneath her desk and hide.

'A real heartbreaker, huh?' he teased, though not unkindly. Then he finally left, whistling *Jingle Bells* as he walked away.

As soon as he was out of sight, Darcy slammed the messy pile of papers onto her desk and glared at Janet. Her friend didn't seem concerned at all. She was slowly nodding, as if she'd seen a vision.

'Yeah. A real heartbreaker,' Janet repeated softly. Her brown eyes gleamed.

'How could you, Janet? He knows that was a lie! Everyone in the office knows that plain old Darcy never has a date. And she certainly doesn't have men lined up around the block for the pleasure of her company!'

Agitated, she leaped to her feet,

towering over her much smaller friend. 'I trusted you! How could you have betrayed me that way?'

Janet didn't respond.

'Janet!' Darcy demanded.

'Keep it down,' someone across the room said, 'I can barely hear with this bad connection.'

Darcy's voice dropped to a hiss. 'What kind of friend are you, Janet Wu?'

'The best kind, Darcy Benton,' Janet said, excitedly. 'Now tell me, all kidding aside — are you really in love with Chase?'

Startled by the blunt question and by Janet's serious tone of voice, Darcy forgot her irritation. She'd thought about her sudden infatuation more than once.

Carefully, she said, 'I was very attracted to him the first instant I saw him. Maybe it was love at first sight or something. But that might have faded with time if I hadn't grown to like him so darn much. I've watched him work like a dog to save this company. You know how he's struggled to keep from filing bankruptcy and tried his best to keep everyone on the payroll.'

'This company is his baby,' Janet said.

'It's more than that,' Darcy disagreed. 'He's fought for his employees as much as for himself. It would have been easier to cut the overhead by cutting salaries, but he wouldn't do that.'

'You don't have to convince me, Darcy. I know he's wonderful. If I hadn't grown up feeling like he was my brother, I'd probably fall for him, too. What I'm trying to find out is this: Do you love him enough to do something about it?'

Darcy eyed her distrustfully. 'What do you mean?'

'Well, I was thinking, there's lots of ways to get across the point that you'd welcome more than an employer-employee relationship. For instance, if you'd act differently toward him, he'd act differently toward you.'

'Spell it out, Janet.'

'Okay. I've never said anything before — '

'Yeah, right,' Darcy grumbled.

'But,' Janet said, ignoring Darcy's complaint, 'you always treat him as if he's a naughty little boy, and you're the old maid teacher ready to rap his knuckles with a ruler.'

'I do not!' Darcy denied, but she knew Janet was at least half correct. Keeping Chase at arm's length was the only way she could keep her sanity when he was around. So she made certain that she was all business when he was near.

'For almost two years, I've watched you worship him from afar. Why haven't you ever tried to get him to notice you?'

'Notice me?' Darcy squeaked.

'Yes, notice you. Like he did a few minutes ago.'

'Oh, sure, Janet. He noticed me all right. He's probably in his office laughing himself silly. A heartbreaker!

Honestly! Don't you ever do anything like that again!'

'Darcy, listen to me. Men want a challenge. They don't want the woman who throws herself at them. They want the woman who won't give them the time of day. Men always want what they can't get.'

'Have you been reading that book of rules I've heard so much about?'

Janet waved her hands in dismissal. 'I don't have to read that book. I could write one of my own. Take my word for it, Darcy, men don't value a woman unless they have to fight for her. It's that old caveman mentality.'

'What has that got to do with what you did?'

'Well, I've got an idea — '

'Oh, no!' Darcy held her hands up. 'Get that look off your face. I am *not* interested in any more of your hare-brained schemes. I shudder when I recall the last brilliant idea you had. We both nearly drowned.'

'Hey, it wasn't my fault the boat

almost capsized before we got to Galveston.'

'You're right. It wasn't your fault a squall blew in. And it wasn't your fault the jerk who rented you the boat forgot to gas it up. I promised myself if I ever got back to solid ground that I would never let you talk me into anything again.'

'Hey, that plan worked, my friend! Did I or did I not get that gorgeous engineer?'

'Yeah, you got him, but you dumped him after two months. You fall in and out of love so fast I'm surprised you don't have whiplash,' Darcy said.

Janet's ginger-brown eyes sparkled mischievously. 'Even so, that brilliant plan worked, and so will this. Confucius says — '

'Confucius? I don't care if you are Chinese, Janet Wu! You don't have any more ancient Chinese wisdom than I do. You grew up on a ranch just west of here!'

'Darcy, just shut up and listen! I'm

trying to tell you how to get Chase's interest.'

'No offense, Janet, but I don't want to trick Chase into dating me. So I'll thank you to stay out of my affairs.'

Janet hooted. 'What affairs? You haven't ever had one! And don't look down your nose at me. You might be taller than me, but you don't intimidate me.' Her head bobbed to emphasize her words.

'Darcy, I've seen you stare at Chase like a starving orphan with her nose pressed against a bakery window. When you think no one is looking, you devour the man with your eyes.'

'I do not!' Upset, Darcy began straightening the pile of pages. Her hands shook as she sorted and stacked. 'You're seeing things.'

Janet gave a distinctly unladylike snort. 'Yes, you do, but don't worry. I'm the only one who's noticed. Everyone else is fooled by your disdainful airs. I must be the only one smart enough to figure out that your abrupt manner is just a defense against the attraction you feel for him.'

The blush deepened on Darcy's cheeks. 'Sometimes I think I'll go crazy if I have to work here the rest of my life. I think about quitting, but the idea of not seeing him is worse than the torture of being around him and knowing he'll never be mine.'

'Well, then, do something about it!'

'Do what? I couldn't get that man interested in me if I came in here stark naked.'

'You'll never know until you try.' Janet grinned. 'I've told you before, you're tall and large-framed, but perfectly proportioned, and you have beautiful posture. You move with quiet grace.'

Darcy glanced at the disordered papers she'd dumped on her desk. 'Sure I do.' She grinned wryly.

'Except when Chase is around.' Janet agreed, her eyes twinkling. 'It's all that repressed sexuality. You need to enlist in the war between the sexes. You've certainly got the ammunition to be a player,' Janet urged, mixing analogies with aplomb. 'Do something before it's too late.'

'Do what? You've seen the women Chase dates. Assuming I could string together ten words in his presence without putting my size ten foot in my mouth, how do I compete with those women? They're all gorgeous and sophisticated. And rich.'

'Don't be dense.' Janet waved her small hands. 'You've got the right equipment. You just need to learn how to use it.'

Darcy folded her arms and drawled, 'What do you suggest I do? Sign up for Female Equipment Utilization 101?'

'Quit with the sarcasm. You are, what they call in modeling circles, statuesque. You've got tons of potential, kiddo. Why that mass of dark brown hair is incredible if you'd just wear it down.'

'I can't come waltzing in here with my hair hanging down to my behind,'

Darcy protested.

'Why not? It would surely get Chase's attention. I've never met a man yet who wasn't crazy about long hair. And your eyes!'

'What about them?' Darcy asked reluctantly.

'They're a lovely gray, but no one can see them because you hide behind those gigantic glasses. You don't even need glasses except for reading.'

When she stepped toward Darcy as if to remove the black-rimmed spectacles, Darcy jerked out of reach. 'Leave my glasses alone.'

'And then there are your clothes.' Janet shuddered.

Darcy's lips pinched into a scowl. 'What's wrong with presenting a professional appearance in the office?'

'Nothing, except nobody wears those shapeless suits and bow ties anymore. You're the only one here who dresses like this.'

Darcy knew that. Her clothes had become part of her armor, just like her square-framed glasses and the tight bun of hair coiled at the back of her neck. She felt safe in her disguise.

'If just once you'd come to the office with your hair down and in a decent dress, maybe a little makeup, you'd have every man here salivating — including Chase Whitaker.'

'Even if what you say is true, I still can't compete with his women. They're rich. They have brains, beauty, and more sophistication in their little finger than I have in my whole body. They're experienced in ways that I'll never be.' Darcy shook her head in despair. 'I haven't even had a date since you fixed me up last year — and that was a disaster.'

Janet nodded regretfully. 'Little Billy.'

'With the forty hands,' Darcy added. Depression, as gray as the winter day outside, settled over her. 'Forget it, Janet. I know there's no way Chase will ever see me as anything except the clumsy girl who runs accounting. Just watch. He'll show up at the party with someone like Claudia Longvale on his arm. She's the type he dates.'

Janet nodded absently. 'Yes, Claudia is his usual type. What a package of beauty, brains, and ego. And she does know how to play the game.'

Feeling really down now, Darcy said, 'She's exactly the kind of woman Chase is attracted to, plus she's the daughter of one of his investors. In fact, he probably will take her to the party,' she said, trying to sound matter-of-fact about the situation when she really wanted to cry.

Darcy finished arranging the last page, glad she'd had that to occupy her hands. 'Now, Janet, let's forget all this emotional nonsense,' she said, forcing her voice to be light, 'we've both got work to do.'

Janet launched herself off Darcy's desk. 'You're absolutely right, Darcy. I've got a ton of things to do. Got to run. Later!'

'Janet, wait!'

When her friend turned to look at

her, Darcy asked in a low tense voice, 'You're not going to do anything else, are you?'

'What do you mean?' Janet asked, eyes wide and innocent.

'I mean it. Don't do some crazy thing that will embarrass me. Please?'

'Darcy, would I do that?'

'Janet?' Darcy's voice warned sternly. 'I mean it.'

Janet giggled. 'You're being paranoid, Darcy. What could I possibly do?'

3

Janet held the receiver to her ear and kept her eyes on the hallway. Timing was everything if this was to work. Just as she saw Chase enter her field of vision, she began her charade.

'No, you've got to quit calling. I'm sorry, Tom,' she improvised, speaking so loudly that Chase couldn't help but hear. 'Darcy doesn't mean to be heartless, but she doesn't want to see you again.'

Janet paused, noting that Chase had stopped. 'She warned you that she likes to play the field.' She paused again. 'Okay, I'll tell her you still love her. Bye now.'

Janet hoped that wasn't laying it on too thick. Replacing the phone in the cradle, she glanced up. Her almond-shaped eyes rounded in pretended dismay. 'Oh, I didn't see you there, Chase.'

'Was that about Darcy?' Chase stood in front of her desk, an empty coffee cup dangling from his fingers.

Janet controlled her urge to giggle. She sighed dramatically. 'Yes. I don't know how I get stuck with talking to these lovesick guys after Darcy dumps them.'

'Lovesick?'

'Yeah, that's the only way I can describe those poor guys. I feel sorry for them, but no matter how infatuated they are, Darcy won't give them a second chance. Once she moves on, that's it. There's no going back.'

'You mean this happens often?' Incredulous blue eyes stared at Janet.

'Too many times, if you ask me. I wish Darcy would settle down, but she just continues to leave a trail of broken hearts wherever she goes.' Janet shrugged eloquently. 'It's really not her fault. The men just won't leave her alone.'

'Darcy?' Chase shook his head in disbelief. 'Darcy Benton? Our accountant, right?'

Janet wanted to laugh at the stunned expression on his handsome face. It was working. Why hadn't she thought of this before?

'Yes, our very own Darcy. She tries to be discreet, I know, but — ' Janet's voice trailed off. Then, as if in surprise, she asked, 'Wait a minute. Chase Whitaker, don't tell me you haven't seen through her disguise?'

'Her *disguise?*' he asked carefully, looking more confused than ever. He set his cup down on Janet's desk and leaned toward her. 'Exactly what do you mean — her disguise?' he repeated, brows arched.

'Oh, Chase, that's rich.' Janet chuckled merrily. 'Do you mean you haven't noticed . . . ?' Expertly, she played her role, laughing as if his supposed ignorance was terribly funny.

Still chuckling, she picked up a drilling report and pretended to read it. Just loud enough for him to hear, she murmured, 'And Darcy was afraid you were on to her.'

Chase stood and looked over the low walls of the cubicles. Janet stood, her eyes following his gaze down the long room to Darcy's office. 'I don't get it. Are you sure this is true?'

'Would I make up a story that wild?' Janet laughed, delighted that he was thinking about Darcy in a whole new way. 'That's even beyond my imagination, wouldn't you think?'

'Yeah. I guess so.' Chase grinned.

'You'd never suspect she had a wild streak as big as the Rio Grande, would you?' Janet asked shrewdly.

'No,' Chase agreed, shaking his head. Janet knew what he was thinking as he watched Darcy leave her office. The dowdy dress-for-success suit made it difficult to determine if her friend wore a size ten or a size twenty. The tight bun made her appear severe. The black-rimmed glasses and the lack of makeup — even lipstick — created a picture of an unemotional, no-nonsense woman.

Janet sighed. She really had her work

cut out for her, she thought, as she viewed Darcy through Chase's eyes.

*   *   *

Though he tried hard, Chase couldn't keep his mind on the Pinto Flats proposal. His curious nature was intrigued by what he'd discovered about Darcy. He'd tried, but he just couldn't see anything different about her. She looked the same as she had the day he'd hired her.

Puzzled by the disparity between what he saw and what Janet had told him, he decided that maybe he should take a closer look. He tossed aside the papers and headed to her cubicle.

As he stepped into her office space, Chase saw Darcy push her chair back and cross her legs. Her gray pleated skirt slid up, showing several inches of shapely thigh. Odd, he'd never noticed her legs before. Her incredibly long legs, he corrected mentally.

'Excuse me, Darcy,' he said, then

wondered suddenly what else to say.

'Oh, uh, Mr. Whitaker,' Darcy mumbled, looking up. Her hands swiftly tugged her skirt down. 'I've got that expense forecast for the workover rig in Eastland County you asked for.' She shuffled papers on her desktop.

'Oh. Uh, yeah,' he said, seizing the excuse she gave him. Intently, he peered at her face, trying for the first time to see beyond the heavy glasses. With surprise, he noted that she had lovely high cheekbones. And the shape of her mouth was wide and sensuous. Hmm. He'd never noticed her mouth before, either.

Darcy fished a manila folder out from the stacks on the desk and handed it to him. Chase sat in the other chair and pretended to study it when in fact, he couldn't get past the thought of her mouth. Bemused, he watched her remove her glasses and lay them on the desk in front of her. With her eyes closed, she rubbed her forehead between the dark curving brows.

'What's the matter? Headache?' Chase asked. He didn't know what possessed him, but he suddenly wanted to soothe the tension away from her normally placid features.

He laid the folder aside and moved behind her. Placing his hands on her shoulders, he kneaded the tense muscles.

'You're tied in knots,' he said, moving his thumbs around and around and up to the base of her neck. Her skin felt warm and smooth beneath his fingers and incredibly soft. Stray tendrils of hair were a whisper of silk against his hands.

She sighed. The sound skimmed along his nerve endings. Unnerved, Chase managed to continue the kneading motion. If he stopped, he was pretty sure his hands would tremble.

'Oh,' Darcy murmured, 'that . . . feels . . . wonderful.'

All the tiny hairs on his body stirred in response. He forgot that they were in the office — and that a dozen people were nearby. His eyes saw only the incredibly soft, creamy skin of her neck. Desire shot through his body.

Really flustered now, his hands stilled. For a moment, neither said anything. The piped-in music seemed to recede, making him wonder if she could hear the riotous beat of his heart. His hands felt as if every nerve ending were attuned to the warm, satiny skin beneath his fingertips. If touching her neck aroused him, what would it be like to slide his palms up her long legs?

Beads of sweat broke out on his forehead and alarm bells clanged in his head. He looked at his hands as they began to slide, millimeter by millimeter.

Abruptly, Chase came to his senses. What was he doing? His hands jerked away as if her skin had seared his palms. Was he insane?

Darcy's eyes flew open. She jerked around in her chair, bumping into Chase and knocking him off balance. He grabbed at the arms of her chair to keep from falling to the floor. That action brought his face within inches of her own. Her startled eyes looked into his and Chase felt an unexpected thrill.

He must have been blind, he decided, never to have noticed that her eyes were the color of wood smoke with the irises ringed by a band of black. Thick dark lashes fringed her beautiful eyes. He was bewitched. Her gray eyes lured him, drawing him into their depths. It wouldn't be a hardship to spend a few hours gazing into her eyes.

'Are you trying to sweep me off my feet, Darcy?' he finally asked, forcing a laugh. Even to his ears he sounded as if he'd just finished running a marathon.

'No,' breathed Darcy, 'I was — you startled me.'

His forehead wrinkled. 'Sorry.' Suddenly confused, he backed away. He'd never laid a hand on any of his women employees before. Agitated, Chase flushed. Office romances weren't his style.

'I apologize. I hope I haven't offended you.'

Darcy shook her head. 'No, of course not.'

'I didn't mean anything by it,' he said stiffly, ignoring the small voice inside that mocked him.

Sure you didn't!

Chase felt as if he teetered on the brink of a steep precipice. Should he look into her eyes again, he knew he'd tumble over the edge. Uncertain what his fate would be if that happened, he decided not to take the leap. He rushed away without another word.

★ ★ ★

Janet, utterly delighted, ducked back into her office before Chase saw her. Her plan had worked! And it had been so easy! She kicked back in her chair, propped her booted feet on the desk, and stared at the ceiling, searching for inspiration.

What should she do next?

When Darcy walked by on her way to the file room, Janet smiled. She knew

Darcy intended to hide out in the file room while she analyzed what had happened. That was part of Darcy's problem. She analyzed things to death and never acted spontaneously.

If left to her own devices, Darcy might truly be in danger of becoming a dried-up old maid. Janet didn't intend to let that happen. What she planned next might be underhanded, but it was for Darcy's own good. She moved the pile of papers away from her phone and looked for the Yellow Pages. She found the nearest florist, and placed an order.

Hanging up, she began to hum *Jingle Bell Rock*. She had an hour to kill. She just hoped that what happened next would have even more dramatic results.

4

At four o'clock, a delivery boy swaggered into the offices of Sunbelt Oil. A draft from the open door fluttered the silver icicles on the tall Christmas tree in the lobby.

'Man, it sure is cold outside,' he said, shaking his head vigorously. Raindrops flew from his crown of black curls. He pulled a piece of paper from the inside pocket of his red ski vest and read, 'Flowers for Désirée Benton.'

'We don't have a Désirée Benton,' Nita Muller, the receptionist, replied, looking up from the Christmas cards she was signing. Her eyes focused on the plastic-shrouded floral arrangement. They gleamed with curiosity. 'Do you mean Darcy Benton?'

'I don't know, lady. I was just told to take these to Désirée Benton at Sunbelt Oil.'

47

'How interesting,' Nita murmured. 'How very interesting. Just a minute, young man.'

She punched in Darcy's extension on the console.

★ ★ ★

The phone on Darcy's desk rang. Janet, who had it staked out, grabbed it on the second ring.

'I'll get her, Nita,' she said, experiencing a moment's misgiving. She hadn't thought about the office gossip's necessary participation in this little scheme.

Nita had little liking for Darcy. Nita, who had been a bookkeeper before, felt that she should have been promoted to the position Darcy had been hired to fill — even though she didn't have an accounting degree and no oil and gas experience.

Oh, well, Janet thought, what harm could it do? She punched the hold button and hurried to the file room where Darcy was still hiding. Chase's door was open wide. Excellent! He couldn't avoid eavesdropping.

'Darcy, there's somebody here with flowers for you. At least, I think they're for you. Isn't your middle name Désirée?'

Darcy came to the doorway. She stuck her pencil in her bun. 'Who would send me flowers? And who knows my middle name?'

Janet slyly removed the pencil from Darcy's bun as she followed Darcy to her desk.

Seconds later, the cute delivery boy strutted in. 'Désirée Benton?' When Janet pointed to Darcy, he whipped the covering from the arrangement with a flourish and handed a vase of beautiful pink roses to Darcy.

'Way to go, Darcy,' one of the dozen men in the big open office called from his cubicle.

Darcy looked at the roses. 'There must be a mistake,' she said even as she signed for the delivery. Bewildered, she placed the gorgeous arrangement on the corner of her desk. Her fingertips gently stroked the velvet-soft pink petals.

The boy stood a few seconds, then shrugged and sighed loudly. He turned to leave, grumbling, 'Surprised women never tip.'

'Who could have sent me flowers?' Darcy murmured.

Janet pulled the tiny envelope from the bouquet and handed it to Darcy. 'Read the card. Then you'll know!'

Darcy laughed. 'You're right. I guess that would be the easiest way to find out.' As she read the message, she frowned. 'Now I know these are for someone else.' She read aloud, 'Pink roses remind me of your petal-soft lips.'

'How romantic!' Janet exclaimed, satisfied to see Chase approaching.

'Flowers from an admirer, Désirée?' he asked, his voice uncharacteristically curt. Darcy blushed beneath his scrutiny.

'Who are they from?' he demanded.

'I don't know,' Darcy murmured, her eyes admiring the roses.

'May I?' Not waiting for permission, Chase pulled the card from her limp fingers and read the mushy sentiment aloud. His lip curled in a sneer. 'What is the guy, a poet?'

Darcy frowned. Why was Chase acting so antagonistic, she wondered. She nodded, confused by his attitude. Then she shook her head. Suddenly she became aware of the intensity of his gaze. The way he studied her mouth made her think he was trying to determine if her lips were really as soft as rose petals. But that couldn't be true.

'Désirée, that's a beautiful name,' Chase said, his gaze on her wide gray eyes. He reached out and stroked one of the roses. Darcy tingled.

His eyes dropped to her mouth. Her lips seemed suddenly dry. She wet them with her tongue. The pupils of his sapphire blue eyes dilated, making his eyes appear an even darker blue.

Janet's voice brought Darcy back to reality. 'Well, which of your current admirers do you think they're from?'

Darcy couldn't focus on Janet's question. She frowned, not wanting the moment to end, but it did when Chase said gruffly, 'Let's get back to work. The day's not over yet.'

With a lingering look at Darcy, he said, 'Now, Miss Benton, if you don't mind.' Then he stalked from the room.

'What's got into him?' Darcy asked, surprised at Chase's surliness. She retrieved the florist's card and read it again. 'These couldn't possibly be for me. Janet — ?'

'Got to go,' Janet said. 'I need to fax the info on that dry hole in Taylor County to Bob before I leave for the day.'

'Janet, wait — ' Darcy began.

'No time, Darcy.' Janet dashed away, leaving Darcy gawking in confusion at the card.

★ ★ ★

Chase shut the door to his office and collapsed onto his leather chair, wondering what the hell was wrong with him. He'd actually wanted to taste Darcy's lips to see if they were as soft as those pink rose petals. They certainly looked as if they could be.

'Désirée,' he said softly, savoring the name that suggested champagne and moonlight — woman and desire. It wasn't a name he'd have attached to Darcy Benton.

If someone had told him this morning that by four o'clock he'd want to kiss the head of his accounting department, he'd have recommended they see a good therapist.

Chase grinned ruefully. Just thinking about Darcy's full lips, soft and natural without a trace of lipstick, made him react in a way he'd never expected. He couldn't stop wondering how her mouth would feel beneath his.

'You've finally lost it, Whitaker,' he told himself, glad no one was around to witness what must be a foolish grin lifting the corners of his mouth. His brain must have been addled by all the late nights. Or lack of sex was playing tricks on his libido.

For a guy who had a reputation as a ladies' man, he'd led a nearly monastic existence for so long that he couldn't remember the last time he'd been with a woman. In fact, he hadn't even thought about sex in months. Saving his business had been his top priority. Obviously, abstinence must have affected his brain if he was beginning to find the staid Miss Benton this attractive.

Chase rubbed his fingertips together, remembering how Darcy's skin had felt. Just touching her had his blood pounding through his veins. And her mouth! He groaned when he thought of her full, sensuous lips. Yep. That must be what was wrong with him. He'd succeeded in saving his company but had lost his personal life somewhere along the way. Shaking his head in amusement, he picked up the Pinto Flats proposal.

A moment later his intercom buzzed quietly. When he heard who was on the line, he groaned. He didn't want to talk to Claudia Longvale right now. She was the only one he'd dated in recent months, and that had just been to keep an eye on her as a favor to her father, Jack. He was tired of baby-sitting the spoiled debutante. He wondered if Jack knew that his daughter was having an affair with one of the lawyers at Longvale Petroleum.

'Hello, Claudia,' he said. While Claudia purred at him in the sexy voice she affected, he pictured Darcy without glasses — huge smoky eyes surrounded by thick, naturally dark lashes. With eyelashes like that, she had no need of mascara and all that other stuff women troweled onto their faces.

'Chase, you're not listening to me,' Claudia complained.

'Yes, I am,' he lied, suppressing the laugh that welled inside when he tried to imagine Claudia Longvale without makeup. Of course, Claudia and Darcy were complete opposites. Or were they? He thought back over what Janet had said.

Suddenly, his attention snapped back to Claudia. 'What did you say?' He sat up straighter.

'I said I'm not very happy that you're ignoring me. We haven't been out in ever so long.'

Irritation crept into his voice. 'Sorry. I've been busy. So have you, I'm sure.'

Chase stared out the window at the icy drizzle that coated the long-needled pines and wondered what Claudia really wanted.

'Aren't you going to ask me to your company party?' Claudia demanded. Chase could almost see her pout. He suddenly thought of Darcy. Who was to be her escort? Maybe he should keep his options open, he thought.

'Hey, if you want to come to Sunbelt's party, come. The more the merrier. Bring a date if you want. In fact, bring that lawyer you've been seeing — Victor Santos, isn't it?

Another mouth to feed won't make a difference.'

'You jerk!' Claudia said.

He grinned when she slammed the phone down. Maybe he should ask Darcy to the big Christmas party. He tried to picture her in an evening gown, but the image wouldn't materialize. Could she really be the party girl that Janet said she was?

Tiredly, he yawned. All those long hours and hard work seemed to have caught up with him. He really did need some rest and recreation. Maybe Darcy was just what he needed, a woman who knew the score and wanted what he wanted — some intelligent company and a little hot sex. As he thought of Darcy, he pictured her mouth. Make that a *lot* of hot sex.

★　★　★

Darcy couldn't keep her mind on her work. Each time she started adding a column of figures, her eyes glided to

Chase's closed door. Then she imagined him all over again, stroking the rose petals and staring at her lips. Part of her suspected he'd wanted to kiss her. Another part pooh-poohed that fanciful notion. Why would he want to kiss plain old Darcy when he had a beautiful blonde like Jack Longvale's daughter at his beck and call?

Office gossip said that Chase and Claudia were having a hot affair. Darcy's heart ached at the thought of another woman in his arms.

Resolutely, she focused on the expense reports. At least in her work she never was racked by feelings of inadequacy. Three hours later, when she initialed the last one, she yawned, stretching her arms overhead. Everyone had gone home. Like most evenings, she was alone in the office, except for Chase, who shared her propensity for overtime.

Darcy cleared her desk and locked up. Burdened with the vase of roses, she opened the outside door and stepped into the gusting wind. Gasping, she ran to her little blue car and headed home to her apartment.

Twenty minutes later, spurred by slivers of sleet, Darcy dashed upstairs. Teeth chattering, she slammed the door and dropped her purse on the oak bench nearby. She headed to the bedroom, wanting only to change from the severe suit into some warm, comfortable clothes. She paused in the living room long enough to set the roses on the ebony baby grand piano in the corner.

The apartment was so quiet she could hear the sound of her steps on the thick carpet. Sometimes, she thought she could hear her own heartbeat in the silence. With each month that passed, the yawning solitude seemed to expand, though she'd filled her life with friends and family and work, always work.

Recently she had begun to notice the too-neat, too-clean, too-silent apartment. She swallowed the sudden lump in her throat. How dumb to be the oldest cliché in the world — a single woman in love with her boss.

Living alone in itself did not make her lonely. But wanting a man she couldn't have *did*. She'd started thinking that it was time to put away her silly fantasy.

Glad to trade her business suit for faded, worn jeans and an old flannel shirt, Darcy removed the pins from her hair and brushed its long length. Surely there must be another man out there who would interest her. Maybe she'd find him at the supermarket tonight.

Her lips twisted. Yeah. Fat chance.

⋆ ⋆ ⋆

Chase thought about Darcy as he cleared his desk that evening. If it wasn't for those revealing glimpses he'd had this afternoon, he'd have bet his last dollar that Darcy Benton was working on being the world's oldest living virgin. But no woman with a mouth like hers could be an innocent at her age.

Chase fantasized about kissing her, tasting her, feeling her lips beneath his. That bit of visualization was easy. Could she really be as wild as Janet said? Somehow, he hoped not, even though he wasn't interested in a permanent commitment.

It's not as if he wanted to marry her — or anybody. He just wanted to kiss her. That would probably be enough to satisfy his curiosity. But his body tightened with desire as he imagined kissing Darcy. No, kissing Désirée. It might take more than one kiss to satisfy him, he thought suddenly.

The phone buzzed as he turned out the lights. He picked it up and heard his mother's voice. He smiled into the darkness. Lucy Whitaker sounded and looked exactly like what she was, a woman who'd taught kindergarten for thirty years.

'Dad and I thought we'd come to town tomorrow to do some last minute

Christmas shopping. How about I fix you a good old-fashioned breakfast in the morning?'

Chase rolled his eyes, knowing what that meant.

Without waiting for his response, his mother said, 'We'll be at your place at seven.'

He groaned. His mother sometimes acted as if he were still a little boy.

The only breakfast-type food he had at home was a box of toaster pastries. He could imagine her expression when she saw that and the six-pack of beer in the fridge. He'd have to endure another well-meaning lecture on the importance of good nutrition. And from there she'd segue into how much longer married men lived, on average, because they had someone to look after them.

Chase didn't want to have to listen to that again. He'd have to stop at the supermarket on the way home.

5

Wind-driven rain blew through the supermarket's automatic door when it opened. Darcy stood aside as a man wheeled out a shopping cart piled high with cases of soda and beer. She sniffed the air, delighting in the evergreen scent of the fresh firs and spruces imported from the Northwest. Just walking through the lane of Christmas trees near the entrance lifted her spirits.

San Antonio in winter, contrary to most people's misconceptions, could be — and often was — cold and wet. Darcy stepped into the warm interior and brushed the mingled sleet and rain from her pile-lined denim jacket.

'Excuse me, miss, you're blocking the doors!' A tired voice broke into her reverie.

'Oh, sorry.' Darcy shrugged her shoulders and grinned. She tapped her index finger on her forehead and said, 'Daydreaming again!' Stepping aside, she watched the woman push her packed cart through the door.

The muted chatter of computer cash registers and the babble of hurried shoppers greeted her, along with the unmistakable melody of *Frosty the Snowman* from the ceiling speakers.

Darcy loved the holiday season better than any other time of the year — from the shopping malls with the giggling crowds of children waiting to see Santa to the neighborhood supermarket decorated with shiny tinsel. She didn't even mind hearing the endless rendition of Christmas carols. Darcy began to hum along with the canned music, determined to feel cheerful.

The holidays had taken a backseat to all the reports that Chase had needed. Because she knew that a lot was riding on the Pinto Flats project, she hadn't complained but had pitched in and worked even longer hours without complaint. Somehow, Christmas felt different this year. Just knowing that she wouldn't be with her family seemed to put everything out of kilter.

When her oldest brother, Marc had been transferred to France for two years, she hadn't believed her parents would actually make good on their wish to visit him during Christmas, but they had left last weekend.

Royce, the next oldest, was spending the holidays with his wife's family in New York, and that left Bruce the Bachelor, as she called him. He was the closest to her in age, and usually a pain in the rear, but he too had abandoned her. Bruce, a San Antonio cop, was pulling duty in place of one of his married friends. Darcy knew it was nice of him to do it so his friend could be home with his wife and kids, but she still felt disgruntled about it. Even Janet was going to be away on a ski trip with her family.

The clang of the Salvation Army bell outside in the frigid night reached her ears. With a shiver, Darcy thought of the poor bell-ringer with his red nose that looked a near match for Rudolph's. She'd make sure to put her change, and a bill or two, in the red bucket on her way out.

Darcy refused to let herself dwell on the atypical Christmas that lay ahead. She would not be lonely, she resolved. She'd have a perfectly lovely Christmas. She'd make it a quiet, peaceful celebration — a time of meditation and solitude.

Adjacent to the lines of rain-spattered steel carts was an alcove crowded with arcade video games. Darcy stopped in front of her favorite game and dug in the pocket of her tight jeans for her stash of quarters. Wiping her palms on the faded denim that hugged her long legs, she dropped her quarter in the slot, and grasped the joystick.

The euphoria of pitting her reflexive skills against the electronic brain infused her cheeks with color. Expertly she dodged through the dungeons and mazes. Unconsciously, she lunged and feinted as she fought to defeat the dark forces of the fantasy world. Her hair swung loosely around her face as she lost herself in the excitement of the game.

* * *

Chase groaned when he saw the lines at the checkout stands. He'd be stuck in the supermarket until midnight! He wheeled a shopping cart toward the produce.

'No! No! No!' a woman exclaimed.

Chase heard the electronic sound of doom and chaos. He looked over at the video arcade where a woman stood, patting her pockets — for more quarters, obviously. He studied her tall frame, admiring the very feminine way she filled out her ancient jeans. A dense cloud of dark hair hung down to her waist. That hair! He'd never seen anything so beautiful!

When she glanced around, Chase's mouth dropped open. His eyes hurried over her rumpled gold and blue flannel shirt beneath an old pile-lined denim jacket and lingered over the part of her anatomy that the too-tight jeans displayed to perfection. He recognized Darcy Benton, but he could scarcely credit that fact.

He looked again at the long legs in the tight jeans. Impossible! Yet there couldn't be that many women, even in Texas, who could stand eye to eye with him in their stocking feet.

No, after today he shouldn't be surprised at anything he found out about Darcy. He'd been wrong about her being undesirable. He'd certainly spent the greater part of the afternoon fighting the desire to kiss her — to touch her. And he wasn't the only one attracted to her if the note with the roses was any indication. Now, looking at her body-hugging jeans and at the natural pink in her cheeks, he knew he'd been wrong about her being unattractive.

Intrigued by the contrasts between

the plain woman he thought he had known and the woman who stood before him, glowing with the excitement of a simple game, he entered the alcove. Until today, he'd have sworn Darcy even slept in one of those mannish suits she wore.

A lazy grin spread across his face. Had he been wrong! His gaze swept from the sexy mane of hair down her incredible legs. The hot, tight feeling in the pit of his stomach returned in full force. He wanted to run his hands up those long legs and across the seat of her nearly threadbare jeans.

So she liked to play games, huh? Obviously not just video games, he decided, thinking of the games she had played at the office — dressing and acting like a dowdy irritant for two years. Why did she want to hide her body and face? And that magnificent mane of hair. Even her personality, he thought, studying her animated expression. Excitement flushed her cheeks.

Chase sidled up to her, leaned over

her shoulder, and whispered, 'We've got to stop meeting like this, Désirée.'

Darcy screamed, jumped, and turned, all in one motion. She collided solidly with him.

'What the — ?' Chase muttered in the instant before he lost the struggle to maintain his balance.

'Oh, my goodness!' Darcy gasped, grabbing for him. His momentum knocked her off her feet.

They collapsed in a tangle of arms and legs. Chase took the brunt of the fall, landing flat on his back on the cold tile floor with Darcy on top of him. The breath whooshed out of him.

For a second, neither spoke. Chase finally managed a gasp of badly-needed air. He stared into startled smoky eyes. Silky black hair grazed his skin. He raised a hand to brush the dark curtain over her shoulder. His hand lingered, tangling in the soft tresses.

Slowly his body acknowledged the intimate press of hers. Her long length fitted him as if she'd been made just for him. He could no more control the evidence of his desire for her than he could stop the freezing rain from falling outside. He tingled with an electric warmth wherever their two bodies touched, and they touched all the way down.

Staring into her astonished eyes, forcefully aware of her, Chase surrendered without a whimper. His hand curved around the back of her neck and urged her face closer. He raised his head slightly to meet her halfway, his lips hungry for the taste of her trembling mouth. It seemed as if he'd waited forever for the touch of her lips, but he couldn't wait another moment if his life depended on it. His blue eyes drifted closed.

Darcy watched his eyes close and hurried to meet his lips. This was better than any of her daydreams. Desire swept through her like fire consuming dry pine needles. She'd never felt anything so powerful before — as if she'd wither and die if she denied herself the kiss being offered. The room seemed to spin like a crazy carousel as her lips touched his.

'Mommy, Mommy! Look at that lady sleeping on top of that man!'

The piercing voice of the child brought Darcy back to reality in one embarrassed second. Her eyes flew open at the same time Chase's did. She stared into his startled blue eyes and felt a blush begin to flood her face.

'Come away from there this instant, Johnny!'

Darcy watched the young mother lift the giggling child into the seat of the shopping cart.

'I guess we'd better get up before she complains to the manager,' Chase drawled, sifting his fingers through her hair.

Blushing furiously now, Darcy scrambled off him. Unable to make her shaking legs move further, she sat on the floor next to him. Her pulse pounded wildly in her throat. What had got into her? She looked over at him as he pushed himself to a sitting position. What had got into him?

Darcy was dizzy with confusion and disappointment. If only that child had held his tongue a moment longer! She was torn between the desire to flee and the equally strong desire to throw herself on top of Chase and beg him to finish what he'd started.

'Are you okay?' he asked.

'Of course.' She was glad her voice didn't sound as shaky as she felt. With an effort of will, she ignored her weak knees and stood. 'I'm just fine.' Though her fingers shook, she busied herself dusting off the seat of her pants and her legs. She avoided looking at Chase. Maybe he'd just walk away as if nothing had happened.

He stood and a gasp escaped his lips. Concerned, she forgot her embarrassment. 'What is it? Are you all right?'

Gingerly Chase flexed his right leg. Then he rubbed the knee as he moved it back and forth. He bit off an exclamation of pain. 'You're hurt!' she cried.

'No,' he said with a rueful grin. 'It's nothing. Just my bum knee. Acts up every now and then to remind me of my glory days in high school football. I must have twisted it when I fell.'

'I'm so sorry!' Darcy wanted to volunteer to kiss it for him to make it better, but had enough sense left to suppress her ridiculous impulse.

Awkwardly, Chase brushed the dust off his clothes. 'Hey, it'll be fine. I just need to walk the kinks out of it. And it's not your fault. It's mine for startling you. I'm the one who should apologize. I don't know what came over me.'

Me either, she wanted to say, but she settled for another apology. 'That's nice of you to say that, but I feel terrible about this.' She sighed. Would there ever come a time when she could be around the man without feeling — and acting — like a one-woman demolition derby?

'Hey, don't feel bad. It was just one of those things.' When he tried to put his weight on his leg, he winced. 'I won't keep you. I've got to pick up some groceries.' Awkwardly, he limped away.

Darcy hung her head. Why him? Of all the people in the Alamo city, why should he be the one to catch her acting like a silly teenager? She followed his limping progress to the front of the row of shopping carts. The words were out of her mouth before she could think. 'Chase, I mean, Mr. Whitaker, wait a minute.'

'Chase is fine,' he grinned as he turned. 'You know, you're the only person in the office who calls me Mr. Whitaker. Makes me think you're talking to my father. You even call my brother Matt by his first name when he drops by. Why Matt and not me?'

Darcy ignored his question. 'Let me help you, please.' She jerked a cart loose. 'You push the cart and just tell me what you want.' Darcy saw his eyes darken.

'What I want?' His gaze fixed on her mouth. 'Uh, sure. That will work.'

'And save us both time,' she added hurriedly.

They moved at a slow pace down the aisles. Darcy used a loaf of French bread to divide his purchases from hers. To her surprise, she found herself relaxing after a bit and enjoying his company. He soon had her laughing with tales of the cholesterol-laden breakfasts his mother loved to prepare.

'She's not kidding when she says she fixes break-fasts that'll stick to your ribs!' he exclaimed.

'And your arteries!' Darcy laughed.

'You have a wonderful laugh,' he said suddenly. 'I don't think I've ever heard you laugh before. You're always so — so serious at the office.'

Darcy looked away. She couldn't tell him that she wanted him so much that she had to hide it behind her severe facade.

By the time they approached the checkout, Chase was walking normally, his knee apparently no longer hurting. 'Oh, I forgot oranges,' he said, turning toward the produce aisle.

Winking at Darcy, he whispered, 'Look, there's Santa.' He pointed at a portly, white-bearded man in a red plaid flannel shirt and red corduroy pants held up by candy-cane striped suspenders. The man even wore heavy black boots that looked capable of tramping through snowdrifts.

Darcy giggled. 'All he needs is a red cap with a white pom-pom.' Chase pushed the cart past the elderly man who looked up from the cranberries he was bagging. He beamed at them.

'Don't you want to tell Santa what you want for Christmas while I get the oranges?' Chase teased, as he tore off a plastic bag and began filling it.

'If only that's all it took to get what you want.' Darcy sighed to herself. She pushed the cart forward.

'Pardon me, miss?'

Darcy turned to the elderly gentleman but didn't stop her forward progress. 'Yes, sir?'

'I wondered if perhaps you could tell

me how to cook these danged cranberries — oh dear! Look out!'

Too late, Darcy turned, just in time
to see her cart strike a mop bucket that
someone had carelessly left in the
middle of the floor. Dirty water
splattered in all directions. She tried to
steer the cart away. Her left foot turned
and a sharp pain nipped at her ankle.
Then there was nothing between the
bottom of her feet and the floor but air.
Darcy landed hard on her bottom in
the cold gray water.

'Darcy! Are you okay?' Chase asked,
running over to her.

'I — I think so!' She blinked rapidly,
wanting only to crawl under a rock and
hide. This was a nightmare. Dampness
soaked through her jeans to her panties.
She struggled to get up. Pain shot up
her left leg from her ankle. 'Oh, no!'

'What is it?' Chase leaned down to
grab her hands and hauled her easily to
her feet.

'It's my left ankle. I turned it when I
fell.' She stood on one foot and rubbed

the painful joint.

The corners of Chase's mouth twitched. His hands tightened on hers. A smothered sound escaped his throat.

'Don't you dare laugh at me, Chase Whitaker! It's all your fault. Every time I get around you — '

'We're an accident looking for a place to happen?'

'Yes!' But Darcy saw the humor, too. The evening had begun with a mishap and appeared to be ending with one. Grinning ruefully, she said, 'I guess we're a dangerous combination.'

Chase nodded. 'I think you might be right.' He pushed her sock down and bent to feel her ankle.

Darcy gasped at the touch of his fingers on her skin.

'Sorry. I didn't mean to hurt you.'

'That's okay,' she mumbled. She could be tortured and she'd never admit that his touch hadn't hurt her. Rather it had heaped kindling on the smoldering desire that burned within her.

'Can you walk on it?'

'I think so.'

'Good girl!' He looked at the water dripping from her backside and reached for his handkerchief. 'Maybe this will help,' he said, grinning.

Gratefully, Darcy accepted the handkerchief, wiping her hands and even blotting her damp bottom, to little avail. 'I'll return this to you,' she said, stuffing it in her pocket.

'Oh, this whole thing is my fault. Or maybe it's Martha's fault for having to have cranberries this time of night,' the bearded old man dithered.

Darcy had nearly forgotten the funny little man. She caught a suspicious twinkle in his eyes behind gold frame glasses. 'It's okay to laugh,' she said, as she took a few experimental steps. 'I'll bet Martha will even laugh when you tell her about this.'

'Oh, you must know Martha,' the plump man exclaimed. 'Look, son, why don't you carry your wife up front, and I'll push your cart up for you.'

'Good idea,' Chase said, lifting Darcy

into his arms as if she weighed nothing.

'Chase Whitaker! Put me down! I'm quite capable of walking!' Darcy worried that he'd be able to feel the erratic pounding of her heart, clutched to his chest as she was.

'Hush, woman! Don't you know we poor men have to boost our sagging egos by carrying a beautiful woman around once in a while? Besides, my knee is fine now.'

Darcy's protests stilled. Beautiful woman? Her? Even though she knew he was joking, his flattery warmed her heart. Being in his arms was better than she had fantasized.

'Anybody ever tell you you're a handful, woman?' he joked.

'All the time. You have no idea what it's like to grow up and be taller than everybody else in your class all the way through school,' Darcy replied honestly.

'Surely some of the jocks in your school equaled you in height?'

'Yes, but they never looked twice in my direction.'

'Being blind must have been a big handicap,' he quipped.

Darcy stared at him. She wasn't used to such flattery. No wonder he was so popular with women.

By the time they arrived at the checkout lane, she felt as if she might be well on her way to cardiac arrest. Frightened at how easy it was to be comfortable in his arms, she declared gruffly, 'Enough is enough. Put me down or else.'

'Or else what?' Chase teased, but he complied.

Ten minutes later, they'd paid for their groceries and the old man, who introduced himself as Dominick, pushed the cart full of brown paper bags out of the store. Chase and Darcy followed.

No matter how much she protested, Chase wouldn't let her walk without his assistance. He kept his right arm around her waist. At first, Darcy held herself stiffly, but the warmth of his body seeped into hers delightfully.

The rain had stopped, and the sky

had begun to clear, but the wind gusted from the north, sweeping down the hill and howling through the parking lot. Darcy shivered. Chase held her tighter. She gave in to the desire to snuggle close to him.

'There's a blue norther coming in,' Dominick exclaimed with a big smile. 'And it's blown the rain clouds clean away.' The man inhaled deeply. 'It's Christmas weather, kids! Don't you just love it?'

Dominick pointed toward the sprinkling of silver stars in the velvety black sky. 'Look! There's the Christmas star.'

Chase studied the direction in which Dominick pointed. 'I thought that was the North Star.' He unlocked his Cadillac.

'Some might call it that, but I've always called it the Christmas star,' Dominick replied. 'If you wish with all your heart on the Christmas star, your wish will come true.'

Whimsically, Darcy looked at the twinkling point of light in the coal-black sky. What the heck! she thought. Closing her eyes, she wished with every ounce of her being for the one thing that she most wanted in the world.

A moment later, she turned around and discovered that Dominick had put all the paper sacks on the floor behind the front seat of Chase's car. 'Wait a minute,' she said.

Dominick doffed a pretend cap and said, 'Merry Christmas, young lady. May all your Christmas wishes come true.' Then to her amusement, he winked and walked away.

Chase's eyes locked with hers. He was delighted that the Santa look-alike had placed all the groceries in his car. Fate seemed to have played a hand in the way the evening had worked out. He smothered Darcy's protests and escorted her to the passenger side. 'In you go.'

Mesmerized by the crazy events of the night, Darcy didn't even argue. Once seated though, realization hit her. 'Wait! My car's here. I'll drive myself home.'

'I wouldn't hear of it,' Chase said,

buckling the seat belt around her. 'Besides, our little Santa put everything in here, and it's too cold and windy to sort them here in the parking lot.'

'This really isn't necessary,' Darcy tried again.

'You don't live with someone, do you?' His eyebrows snapped together. He didn't like the prospect of immediate competition.

'No, of course not.'

'Good,' he muttered to himself, 'that could complicate things.' At least he wouldn't have to contend with the guy who'd sent the roses tonight. He slammed the door and walked around to his side and climbed in. He'd have to find out who the competition was, though — so he could eliminate it.

'But what about my car?' Darcy pointed at her blue Honda.

'Your car is a stick shift. Right?'

At her nod, he continued, 'You can't drive a stick with a sprained ankle. Popping the clutch will make your ankle worse.'

'But my ankle hardly hurts at all now.'

'But if you drive, it'll start hurting again,' he argued. 'I insist on driving you home and getting you settled. Then I'll separate the groceries.' He didn't wait for further arguments. He turned the ignition key.

'But how will I get to work in the morning?'

'I'll pick you up,' Chase said, entering the busy side street. He liked that idea. At her protesting squawk, he asked, 'And what's wrong with that? It stands to reason if your car is here, then you need a ride to work. If we both shop here, then you must live nearby so it won't be an inconvenience.'

'But I can call a friend to come pick me up.'

'A friend?' Chase didn't like that idea at all. 'I don't think so. I said I'd take you home. I'll be your friend.'

'But you're my boss!'

'Oh, I get it. You keep your professional life and your social life separated. That explains things, I guess.'

Darcy gazed forlornly at her car as he pulled away. 'Yes! No! I mean, what are you talking about?'

'Relax, Darcy, I think I'm beginning to understand everything. Except why I didn't see it before.'

'You're not making a bit of sense, Chase.'

'Come on, you don't have to play that game with me anymore. Just because I'm your boss doesn't mean I can't be your friend.'

Exasperated, Darcy shrugged. 'Fine. You're my friend.'

'Good. Now that we have that settled, tell me how to get to your apartment.'

Chase turned on the heater. Darcy welcomed the blast of warm air. Bewildered by the strange conversation and the bizarre events of the evening, Darcy wondered again if she were dreaming. She directed him to her apartment complex a few blocks away.

'I have a condo about the same

distance from the grocery store in the other direction,' Chase said. 'How about that? All this time we've lived within a couple of miles of each other.'

Maybe I've entered the Twilight Zone, Darcy thought, almost hearing the eerie theme from the old black and white television series. She glanced over her shoulder, half-expecting to see the doleful face of Rod Serling leering from the backseat. Or perhaps this was a parallel existence where fantasies reigned, and your dreams came to life to tease you. Whatever was happening, she was intrigued and excited by it.

Her thoughts returned to the inter-rupted kiss. Was it possible for Chase to be overcome again by the same temporary insanity? Her heart slammed against her ribs at the thought. She stared at the rain-slick streets and clenched her hands to stop their trembling.

Did wishes really come true?

6

Chase thought about the woman who sat next to him as he drove to her home. The sound of the tires on the wet pavement seemed unnaturally loud to his heightened senses.

What a night this had turned out to be. He glanced at Darcy. Her profile was as lovely as an old-fashioned cameo. His brow wrinkled in confusion. Old-fashioned was how he'd always thought of Darcy. That image couldn't be true in light of what Janet had told him.

Hidden beneath that serene portrait was the sensuous, appealing woman he'd held in his arms. She had to be the playgirl that Janet had described. How could two such different women occupy the same body? The more he looked, the more he found her fascinating. It wouldn't be a great hardship to spend hours staring at her.

Then he'd like to spend a few more hours sifting his fingers through her long, dark hair, feeling its texture, inhaling its faint perfume. He remembered the feel of her body pressed against his. He wouldn't mind spending a few hours experiencing that again either. He smiled, recalling her uninhibited laughter earlier in the evening — at her own expense. He couldn't call to mind another woman he'd dated who would have been as quick to see the humor in an embarrassing situation. He chuckled quietly.

'What's so funny?' Darcy asked stiffly, certain that he was laughing at her.

'Oh, it's not funny, just pleasant. I was thinking how different you are from most of the women I know.'

'Oh.' Darcy cringed, wishing he wasn't so candid in making the comparison. She swallowed hard. He was regaining his sanity, she decided forlornly. 'My apartment complex is on the right in the next block.'

He turned at the second entrance as she directed, then parked in the slot her car had occupied earlier.

'Give me your key and I'll go open up,' he said.

Resigned to his gallantry, Darcy complied.

He gathered the groceries in his arms and sprinted up the stairs. Within minutes he was back, scolding her when she opened her door and climbed out. He simply refused to listen when she insisted on walking alone.

To her surprise, he tried to pull her into his arms again, but she would have none of it. Forcing a laugh, she evaded him, not trusting herself to keep her hands off him. 'There's nothing wrong with my ankle, Chase. It feels fine,' she said, starting up the stairs.

'No fair! You shouldn't deprive a man of the opportunity to play Sir Lancelot!' He followed her, acting as if she were going to swoon at any moment.

Surprised, Darcy laughed. 'Is that

who you are? Sir Lancelot?'

'Lancelot is my name. Rescuing damsels in distress is my game,' he sang out.

Darcy giggled. 'Well, I guess you'll just have to go fight a dragon instead. Or live with your disappointment,' she called over her shoulder. 'Because I don't need your assistance.'

'Are you sure?' His voice dropped to a husky whisper as he stepped up next to her and put an arm around her shoulders, ostensibly to guide her the last few feet. They fit together, hip to hip, perfectly.

'I'm not sure of anything tonight,' Darcy murmured, staring into his eyes, wishing his teasing words were sincere.

'Me either, Darcy.' Chase knew he'd have to kiss her or die trying. But not here on the stairs, in the cold. Not with her standing on a sprained ankle.

'Let's get inside,' he urged.

Within minutes, he had her on the couch, legs extended, with a rust-red throw pillow behind her back.

He looked around her living room,

surprised at the lush colors in the decor. The room reminded him of a west Texas sunset — rich rusts, indigo, and fiery gold. He laughed. 'How'd you get that in here?' He pointed to the baby grand piano.

'That's one good thing about having three big brothers.' Darcy told him how the three hulking Benton brothers had hauled the piano up via the balcony.

'I like your place. It's full of warmth and energy,' he called over his shoulder as he walked to the kitchen.

'What are you doing?' she called, listening to the sound of cabinet doors in the kitchen being opened and closed.

'Fixing you an ice bag for your ankle.'

'I don't need it. There's nothing seriously wrong with my ankle.'

Chase ignored her protests and filled a plastic bag with crushed ice from the freezer's dispenser. She might not need it, but it gave him the perfect excuse to stay longer. Why was she so anxious to kick him out? Wasn't she attracted to him, too?

'I didn't know you played the piano,' he said, reappearing, a makeshift ice pack in his hands.

Darcy laughed. 'Both my parents were music majors. I didn't stand a chance of getting out of piano lessons.'

'Do your parents teach?'

'My dad's a band director, and my mom has always given private lessons in piano.'

'Let's get that shoe off.' He bent to unlace her shoes, brushing her hands aside when she tried to do it. He left her sock in place. 'Were you in the band in school?'

Darcy looked away from his eyes. Chase placed the bag of crushed ice against her ankle.

'Oww!' Darcy yelled. 'That's cold.'

'It's supposed to be.' Chase grinned at her. 'Well, were you in the band?'

Darcy nodded. In an embarrassed voice, she mumbled, 'I played a few instruments.'

'A few? You really must be talented. Which ones?'

'Oh, some brass ones.' She mumbled, not wanting to tell him.

'What kind of brass ones?' he persisted.

Darcy fiddled with the ice bag. 'Oh, the trumpet and the trombone.' Her voice dropped to a whisper, 'And the tuba.'

'The tuba?' Chase hooted, rocking back on his heels.

'See, that's exactly why I've never forgiven my dad,' Darcy said. 'All the other girls played dainty things like flutes or clarinets — but not me. I had to play the tuba,' she finished darkly, 'just because I was the tallest in the band.'

Chase smiled. 'Was it a genetic plot on your father's part? Maybe he knew that one day he'd need a beautiful dark-haired girl to play tuba because all the boys in the band would be ninety-pound weaklings.'

His flattering words warmed her heart. 'Well, the part about the boys being weaklings was true. And they were short. It was my freshman year in high school.' She sighed. 'Living in a small town is the pits.'

'Which town is it?'

'My family lives in Vernon, population an even thousand.'

'Let me guess. Your dad has been the band director forever?'

Darcy laughed. 'Just about.'

'Actually, it was pretty funny,' she confessed. 'My mom is so tiny — my brothers and I tower over her. She was mortified when Dad asked me to do it. I don't think she's ever forgiven him either!' Darcy laughed.

Chase laughed with her, enchanted by the picture of a coltish Darcy, probably all legs and arms, carting a big tuba around. He rose from the floor and sat on the edge of the couch facing her. She scooted over to make room for him, but he edged over until his hips pressed against the side of her thigh.

He wanted that kiss he'd thought about all day. One kiss ought to take care of his curiosity about Darcy

Benton. He leaned toward her.

Darcy leaned away from him, an expression of uncertainty in her suddenly pale face. He pressed her gently against the pillows, wanting to savor the moment. His arms encircled her.

'What are you doing?' she whispered, taken aback.

'I'm embracing you,' he whispered back, unable to suppress a smile.

'Why?'

'Because I'm going to kiss you.'

'Oh.' Darcy sat stiffly, her eyes wide with shock. He was still insane, she decided, delighted in the knowledge.

Chase pulled her to him. 'Relax, Désirée,' he murmured, his mouth an inch from hers.

'Are you sure you want to do this?' she asked nervously, not caring that he called her by her hated middle name.

'Very sure.'

'Oh. Okay.'

His lips brushed hers, ever so softly, then hovered a fraction of an inch above her. Their breaths mingled. He could feel the heat rising from her skin. He returned to her lips, nibbling and tasting. Her mouth opened softly as she sighed.

Chase took his time, playing with her soft lips, stoking her desire, but finding his yearning growing with each gentle touch as well. His blood thundered through his veins. Their tongues teased, lingered. When she moaned against his lips, he lost it.

His mouth slanted across hers, starving for all she would give him. He felt her hands sliding up his arms, stroking his shoulders, his neck, his back, caressing him with what could only be desire. The groan that split the quiet came from him, he realized, dazed.

'Oh, yes,' Darcy whispered eagerly. 'Yes, yes, yes!' She'd dreamed of this, but the reality was so much better than her imagination. Her hands wanted to own him, to possess him, for now and for all the minutes of her life.

Chase devoured her mouth, burning

kiss after kiss onto her lips, her cheeks and her neck. Her uninhibited response delighted him. The woman could definitely kiss, he thought, stunned by the fire she ignited in him. Overwhelmed by the force of her passion, he needed more than kisses from her, he realized.

He'd been a fool to think a few kisses would be enough. When he brushed his palms across her shirt-front, she shuddered in response. And so did he. His hands shook. He tasted the softness of her throat and the fluttering pulse there. He wanted to touch her and see her and feel the beauty of her long-limbed body.

'Where's the bedroom?' Chase asked, his voice thick with desire.

* * *

Darcy opened her eyes, jarred back to reality by his question. Her body gloried in the sensations he was arousing, but her mind shrieked a warning.

Bedroom?

Everything was moving too fast. Way too fast. It took every ounce of her willpower to turn her head away when his mouth sought to claim hers again, but she managed. Barely.

Gasping for air, she pushed at him. 'No! Chase, please. No.'

Desire glazed his eyes. He seemed befuddled, as if he didn't understand the meaning of what she'd said. He repeated the word that had brought everything to a screeching halt. 'No?'

His brow wrinkled in confusion. Silently, he searched her face. 'No?' he echoed in disbelief.

'I'm sorry,' she cried. 'I can't! This is too soon.' Darcy looked up at him, surprised that he seemed as lost in the storm of emotion as she. 'I'm not prepared for . . . for this — ' she waved her hand at him. 'I have to say no,' she whispered. 'Please understand.'

Though she'd fantasized for two long years about Chase Whitaker, this wasn't a silly daydream. This was reality, and she needed to think before taking such a drastic step.

After several long silent moments, he sighed and pressed a kiss to her forehead. 'I understand. I'm not prepared either.' He looked at her kiss-swollen lips.

'I'd better leave while I can. I'll see you at eight in the morning,' he murmured, brushing another kiss on her lips.

Startled at his impending departure, Darcy grabbed his lapels and held him. He kissed her again. And again. Within moments, they were lost to all but the sensation of each other's mouths and soft breaths.

Darcy had tried, she told herself distractedly. But her determination to be sensible faded more with each kiss. For once in her life, she wanted to yield to impetuosity. Just this once, she wanted to be guided by passion, not analytical thinking. She loved him. Only him.

Suddenly, Chase jerked out of her

arms. He stood. Darcy stiffened at his rejection. Chase groaned and ran his fingers through his tousled hair. He gasped, 'Darcy, I've got to go now, or I won't be able to in another minute.'

He took a deep breath and grinned ruefully. He kissed the tip of her nose. 'It's best for both of us. Neither of us is prepared for what will happen next.

'Soon,' he promised softly. He pulled her to her feet and held her against him for a long moment. 'Soon,' he whispered again. 'Come on. Walk me to the door.'

Dazed, she did as he asked. 'Goodbye,' she whispered when he stood on the other side of the threshold. She didn't wait to watch him walk away. It hurt too much. Her entire body was quaking like a leaf in a whirlwind. She closed the door quickly and locked it. Then she leaned against the cold steel door to catch her breath and marvel at what had just taken place.

For the first time in her life, she knew the full meaning of desire. Of passion.

She ached with it. No, she throbbed with it. She'd never imagined kissing could be so wonderful.

If the stars weren't still visible in the night sky, she thought, it was because they now filled her eyes.

Yes, she decided dreamily. Wishes could come true.

★ ★ ★

The clouds had rolled in since he'd been in Darcy's apartment, Chase noted. Once again they obscured the stars. He whistled as he skipped down the stairs, feeling like a kid again. It had been months since he'd felt this intensely alive.

Icy rain pelted him as he dashed to his car, but he barely felt it. The only thing he was aware of was the raging desire Darcy had ignited in his body. He must have been blind never to see the passion stirring in her smoky gray eyes. How she could have fooled him for so long amazed him. He brushed his fingers across his lips, recalling the texture of her soft mouth, the shape of her body beneath his hands. She could give lessons in the art of kissing, he decided, touching his lips.

He'd been wrong about so many things about Darcy. For starters, he'd been completely off base thinking that a kiss would satisfy him. A million kisses — even those as tantalizing as Darcy's — wouldn't begin to sate the hunger she'd aroused in him.

Chase grinned, impatient for their next encounter.

7

By seven o'clock the next morning, Darcy had changed clothes six times, poked holes and runs in two pairs of pantyhose, and exhausted the contents of her closet.

The only thing constructive she'd managed to do was find the sample bottle of makeup base she'd received from a door-to-door cosmetic saleswoman. The color didn't match her skin tone very well but it did hide the marks of passion on her throat. If it hadn't been for those faint bruises, Darcy would have been convinced that she'd dreamed up the searing kisses Chase had pressed there.

Scowling at her reflection, she realized that she looked rather like a penguin. She'd never be ready when Chase arrived, she thought, slipping out of the black suit and white blouse. She ran her hands through her disheveled hair and moaned. No matter what combination of shirts and suits she tried, nothing worked. Reluctantly she agreed with Janet. She did need a makeover, especially if it included a new wardrobe.

Defiantly, she pulled a severe long-sleeved black tube dress from the hanger. It was a simple sheath that skimmed her hips and ended at the tops of her knees. She'd never worn the dress to work because she thought it was too short. Now, looking at her reflection, she decided it was as nonsexual as her career suits. In fact, it seemed downright matronly. Darcy felt different this morning and had wanted to *look* different, but Chase would be here shortly, and she wasn't even ready.

Darcy shivered, remembering the hot kisses they'd exchanged. How should she act when she saw him? How did the women he dated act the morning after? Of course, since she and Chase hadn't done anything but kiss, maybe 'morning after' wasn't the right phrase at the moment. Fine, tell that to the butterflies dive-bombing in my stomach, she thought.

'Quit dithering, Darcy,' she told herself. That's what her mother would say if she were here. Glancing at the clock, she saw she only had twenty minutes to figure it all out.

Quickly, she smoothed her last pair of dark hose over her legs, then tidied her messy bedroom. Just as she stepped into a pair of black pumps — no sensible flat shoes today, she'd rebelliously decided — the phone rang. She grabbed the cordless from the night-stand.

'Hello?' she muttered, walking to the bathroom to hunt for her lipstick. She knew she owned at least one.

'Hey, Stretch! You mad at anyone in particular or just the world in general?'

'Bruce, I don't have time to talk now. I'm running late.' Frantically, Darcy rifled through the vanity drawer, determined to wear lipstick today, if she

107

could only find the ancient tube.

'This will only take a few minutes.'

Darcy rolled her eyes. Her brother's definition of a few minutes was vastly different from hers. He acted as if he had all the time in the world. Maybe that's why he was such a successful homicide investigator.

'Call me later at work. Please, Bruce?'

'I have an appointment later. This will only take a few minutes. Mom's right, you do think you're married to that job. Sunbelt Oil won't fall apart if you're not there precisely on the dot at eight o'clock.'

Darcy didn't bother to explain what was really wrong. She'd tried hard to convince her parents and brothers that her career was the most important thing in life. She didn't want them to know how big a lie that was.

'The last time you needed to speak to me urgently was to talk me into buying one of your girlfriends a present, and I quote, 'Be sure it's something that looks like I spent a lot of time shopping for it.''

She ignored his unrepentant laugh. 'What is it now? Another last minute gift for one of your harem?'

'No, you got it wrong. This time I'm going to do you a favor. There's this new guy that I thought you might enjoy meeting.'

'Bruce!' Darcy wailed. 'Why is it that everybody suddenly thinks I need to get fixed up?'

'Hey, take it easy. Just meeting a guy for a cup of coffee or a drink doesn't constitute getting fixed up.' At her derisive snort, he sighed. 'Besides, Mom made me promise to do it.'

'I thought I'd cured her of that.'

'Nope. Just because she doesn't ask you every week if you're dating anyone *yet* doesn't mean she's given up.'

The doorbell rang. Panicked, Darcy interrupted, 'There's my ride, and I'm not ready!'

'When did you start carpooling?'

'I haven't. I, uh, hurt my ankle last

night and had to leave my car at the grocery store parking lot when a, uh, friend, gave me a lift home.'

'How bad is the ankle? Is it the one you broke playing football? Did you go to the doctor?'

The doorbell pealed again. 'No third degree now. I don't have the time. My ankle's fine. Call me later, and I'll fill you in.' Darcy hung up and rushed to the door.

'I'm a little early,' Chase began. He gazed intently at her tangled hair. A slow smile spread across his face, and his eyes darkened. In a low, intimate voice, he said, 'So this is what your hair looks like when you wake up.'

Darcy was mortified. His teasing remark struck a blow to her meager feminine ego. Her hands rushed to smooth her hair, but the unruly mass didn't want to be smoothed. She knew it must stick out in all directions.

'I'm sorry. I'm not quite ready. I got stuck on the phone with Bruce,' she managed breathlessly.

'No problem,' he said, stepping in. 'Who's Bruce?' he asked nonchalantly.

And that was that, Darcy decided, feeling foolish for thinking — hoping — that he would sweep her into his arms. Oh, well, it's probably for the best, she told herself, but her heart didn't agree.

'I'll just be a few minutes. There's coffee in the kitchen if you'd like a cup.'

'Who's Bruce?' Chase asked again.

Darcy ignored the question as she hurried to the bathroom. She blamed the silly tears in her eyes on the tight knot of hair she quickly fashioned, securing it with a few hairpins.

Taking one last look at her reflection, she decided morosely that she looked the same as usual. But that was good. That would help her act normal, not like a starry-eyed teen, she told herself. Last night had been an aberration. This was the cold, clear light of day.

'I apologize for not being ready, Mr. Whitaker.' she said, briskly, putting on her big black glasses.

Chase arched a dark brow. 'Mr. Whitaker?' Carrying two mugs of coffee, he walked toward her. His grin was as lazy as his steps. 'Now, Darcy, that just won't do.' He handed her both mugs and reached up and removed her glasses. Then he folded them and placed them in his suit coat pocket.

'What — ?' Darcy's eyes rounded. 'What are you doing?'

When he grasped her upper arms gently, she nearly dropped the mugs of coffee. 'Mr. Whitaker,' she asked breathlessly, 'what are you doing?'

'Why, Miss Benton, I'm kissing you.' With that his mouth settled on hers.

'Oh!' Darcy exclaimed softly. His smile was the last thing she saw as her eyes drifted shut.

'What's my name?' He teased the corner of her mouth with the tip of his tongue.

'Your name?' Dazed, Darcy tried to figure out what he meant, but her brain seemed to have gone on strike. She couldn't think, could only feel. How wonderful! He was still off his rocker! She smiled.

'Yes, my name. Am I Mr. Whitaker or Chase?'

'You're — you're Chase,' Darcy whispered.

'Excellent, you learn fast,' he replied, taking his cup from Darcy's trembling hands.

Her eyes slowly opened. His satisfied expression — like the cat who has dined on the canary — brought her up short. Suddenly, the logical side of her personality reared its detail-oriented head.

Why was he so infatuated with her all of a sudden? Darcy had no answers to that question. Somehow, she couldn't believe it was because she had wished on a Christmas star. She tried to push her suspicious questions away, but they wouldn't budge. She felt as if she and Chase were playing a game, but no one had bothered to explain the rules to her. Her unease grew.

'Why did you kiss me last night?' she asked.

'Because I wanted to.' Chase's smile showed his dimples and crinkled the corners of his eyes. 'You don't have to pretend any longer, Darcy. I know your secret.'

Darcy blanched. Oh, no. No!

He knew that she was in love with him!

'How,' she swallowed, mortified. 'How did you find out?' She wanted to vanish, just dry up and let the wild winter wind blow her away like a pile of fallen leaves.

'That's my little secret.' He sipped from his coffee cup. 'You make good coffee,' he said.

'Thank you,' Darcy muttered. Finally, she said, 'You seem very blasé about it.'

'About your coffee? Oh, not at all.' He grinned. 'It's important to have a good cup of — '

'No!' Darcy slashed the air with her hands. 'Not about the dumb coffee, about the . . . other.'

'Well, there's no need to get upset about it, is there? You can't help the way

114

you are any more than I can help the way I am.'

She couldn't meet his eyes. 'I promise you it won't affect my job performance.'

Chase threw his head back and laughed. 'Darcy, your job performance is the last thing on my mind right now.'

'I just thought I should make it clear,' she said, speaking more to the floor than to him.

'Well, let me make something clear. Now that I know about it, don't you think you could loosen up a little? Not that I want to advertise an affair around the office. Though I've never dated anyone who works at Sunbelt before, I don't plan on keeping it a secret and doing it clandestinely.'

That brought Darcy's head up. She frowned, 'An affair?' She hadn't thought her heart could pound any harder, but she'd been wrong. 'What do you mean?'

'You don't think we can go back to ignoring each other after last night, do you?' His eyes caressed her. 'Say, you look different today. What is it?'

Darcy wished she had worn one of her baggy suits and her usual flats. She crossed her arms over her chest and tried to shrink. 'Nothing's different. It's your imagination. And as for last night, why can't we just forget? It was just a few kisses.'

'But what kisses!' Chase said. His eyes on her mouth made her insides quiver. 'Kisses were fine last night, but I want more now. Don't you?'

'Like an affair?' Darcy asked, her voice bleak. In all her fantasies, she'd never visualized an affair with him. Her daydreams always took the shape of a marriage and happily ever after — including children, a dog, and a house with a big mortgage, just like other married couples.

Could she ignore that daydream and settle for a love affair with him?

'Why not?' he asked, his voice low and husky.

8

Why not indeed, Darcy wondered, dazed. She couldn't deny that she desired him. Would it be wrong to have an affair with the man she'd loved for so long? Especially when he suddenly seemed so willing. He must care for her if he wanted to make love with her.

'Let's go forward, my sweet Désirée.'

That was another thing, she thought, remembering the flower delivery. The number of people who knew her ridiculous middle name was limited to family and close friends. Chase hadn't known it before yesterday. When he said her name, with that husky, sexy note in his voice, it subtly undermined her will to resist him.

'Your lips are indescribably sweet, but I want more than a few kisses.'

'But what about what I want?' Darcy's fists clenched. She knew she'd never survive an affair with him. When he left her, as he inevitably would, her life would be shattered in a million pieces. She could almost hear her foolish dreams breaking into a million pieces already.

'Why don't you come sit next to me and we'll discuss it?' He patted the cushion next to him.

Darcy shook her head. 'No, I think I'd better stay here.' She knew she had to keep some distance between them.

Chase set his coffee mug on the varnished driftwood coffee table and came to her instead. He gently grasped her chin and forced her to look into his eyes. She didn't resist, but looked deeply, trying to read his thoughts, his intentions. His heart.

'Don't you want the same things I want, Darcy? More kisses?' He kissed her earlobe, sending heat spiraling through her. He kissed the spot on her neck where her pulse throbbed. 'I want to kiss you until you're breathless. Until you moan my name and tell me never to stop,' he whispered against her skin.

'More touching?' His hands spread fire along her back and curved around her waist. Darcy closed her eyes, her breathing ragged.

'Deeper intimacy?' he whispered. 'I want to be so deep inside you that we can't tell where I end and you begin. I want to touch you and kiss you — stroke you until you're weak with wanting.'

Darcy closed her eyes. That shouldn't take more than a second or two, she thought.

'You're really asking me to have an affair with you?' she whispered, ready to surrender if he said the magic words. She clung to the silly hope that maybe he really was in love with her. He must love her if he were proposing an affair. An affair could lead to marriage, couldn't it?

Chase's hand moved up to trace her earlobe. 'Yes, I am. I want you so much that I can't think of anything or anyone but you. I don't think I've ever wanted any woman quite as much. I'm half crazed with wanting you.'

The words hung in the air. They burned into Darcy's brain.

He wanted her!

But what of love? Where was the love to go with that wanting? Frozen in his arms, it occurred to her that this wasn't the way it was supposed to happen. Last night, she had wished that Chase would want her as much as she wanted him. Apparently, her wish had been granted. He wanted her!

How funny! She should have worded her wish more carefully, Darcy thought. Her quirky sense of humor saved her from dissolving in tears. She choked back the hysterical laughter that bubbled in her throat.

'I've always heard to be careful what you wish for,' she murmured.

'What's that?' Chase asked.

'Nothing.' Anger and hurt and a sad amusement at the situation warred within her. He did indeed want her

— but only her body.

Darcy wanted his heart! She wanted to give her love to him, but he didn't want that. He just wanted to go to bed with her. And all his smooth, arousing words couldn't change that fact. Anger gained the upper hand.

'Let me get this straight,' she said, keeping a tight rein on her temper. 'You want to have an affair with me?'

Chase nodded, trying to kiss her again, but she pulled back. He frowned.

'Let me guess,' she said tightly. 'No strings attached, right?'

'Right,' he said, grinning. 'Isn't that the way you want it?'

'Oh, absolutely,' she said, feeling slightly hysterical.

'Great.' His grin broadened.

Darcy seethed. Janet must have told Chase that she was in love with him. Just wait till she got her hands on that woman.

She stoked her anger so that she wouldn't give in to the part of her that said she was a fool to turn him down

— on any terms. Sitting here with him and knowing he wanted her only for sex hurt, but how much more pain would the future bring if she gave in to his casual proposition?

Suddenly, she realized that she valued herself more than to indulge in a cheap affair when what she wanted was marriage. All the fight went out of Darcy. Last night, when she was feeling foolish and lost in the magic of his kisses, was all she'd have of him. That would have to be enough.

'No.' She shook her head to emphasize her decision.

'What do you mean no?' Chase's forehead wrinkled in confusion.

'No, thank you,' Darcy added snidely. Did he think she was so besotted that she'd fall at his feet? Maybe she had more self-esteem than either of them thought she possessed.

'Why not?'

'Because I don't want to.' Darcy rose. 'I think we need to go now,' she said calmly.

'Because you don't want to!' Chase echoed blankly.

For the first time, Darcy saw some real humor in the situation. She had a sneaking suspicion that no one had ever turned Chase Whitaker down before.

Suddenly, she seemed to be the one who was decisive and in charge. She left him sitting on the loveseat while she went to the kitchen and turned off the coffeemaker. Then she got her coat and put it on. When she returned to the living room, he was pacing back and forth.

'We'll be late if we don't leave now,' she prompted.

He scowled. 'So we'll be late. Big deal.' He ran his hands through his hair as if harried and confused.

Darcy couldn't believe her ears. 'You've never been late before!'

'Neither have you,' he said, turning to look at her. Suddenly, he seemed to notice her shoes for the first time. The corner of his mouth quirked up. 'New shoes?'

'No,' Darcy snapped, wishing she hadn't yielded to the impulse to change her appearance. It was all for nothing anyway.

Chase swaggered toward her. 'I like you in heels. I'm not one of these men who feel threatened by a woman who can look him in the eye.'

For once, being reminded of her height didn't bother her. 'Let's go if you've finished analyzing my appearance,' she snapped, determined not to let him get to her.

'Look at it this way. If we're late, it's the first of several new experiences we can share,' he suggested.

'I prefer to think of it as being a blemish on my work record,' she retorted, throwing open the front door.

Chase followed her downstairs. 'I think you're protesting entirely too much.'

Darcy wished he wouldn't crowd her. His nearness agitated her. 'It's a free country. You can think anything you please.'

'I also think I'm going to enjoy changing your mind, Darcy. We are going to have that affair.' He moved in for the kill. 'You're too passionate and hot-blooded to deny yourself the pleasure we can give each other.'

Darcy found it difficult to believe that he was describing her. Passionate? Hot-blooded? Stubbornly, she fought the flood of longing his words prompted. 'Don't be so arrogant, Chase Whitaker. Every man has to take no for an answer occasionally.'

'Oh, arrogance has nothing to do with it, Darcy Désirée Benton. If you really meant no, I'd accept it. Tell me you didn't enjoy our kisses.'

Unable to say a word, Darcy ignored him, but she felt his eyes on her. Did he think just because she was in love with him, that she'd fall into his bed? Well, he had another think coming. She took a deep, calming breath. 'I won't lie to you, I did enjoy them. But that doesn't mean I'm going to have an affair with you so you may as well forget it.'

'You sure are cute when you stick your chin out like that, Désirée,' he said, chucking her on the chin as he walked past. The look on his face plainly said the subject wasn't closed.

'Don't call me that. No one calls me Désirée, not even my mother. And she's the one who stuck me with that ridiculous name.'

Chase chuckled. 'Then that's my special name for you.'

'I don't want you to have a special name for me.' Her lips tightened. She just wanted him to leave her alone — before her resolve weakened.

I'll just have to stay out of his way, she thought, sliding into the passenger seat as he held the door open to his car. That shouldn't be too hard. She'd had plenty of practice avoiding him during the last two years.

Darcy didn't say anything else until they pulled onto the street. Then, determined to act as if nothing were different in their relationship, Darcy asked, 'I thought your mother was cooking breakfast for you this morning.'

'Oh, she did. I couldn't take the usual investigation into who I was dating, was it serious, and so on. Sometimes Mom drives me up a wall with her interest in my love life.'

Did his parents approve of Claudia Longvale? Darcy sighed, suddenly depressed.

Aloud she said, 'I know what you mean. My mom is the same way. I just found out that she's drafted one of my brothers into finding a suitable man for me.'

'You don't need a suitable man. They're boring. You've got me instead.'

'Well, thank you very much, but I don't want you,' Darcy said.

After that, they rode in silence until they reached the parking lot of Sunbelt Oil. As Chase parked in his reserved space, Darcy murmured her thanks and got out of the car quickly. Shivering, she pulled her coat closer.

Chase caught up with her. 'Hey, what's the big hurry?' He grasped her elbow, forcing her to slow her steps.

Self-preservation, she wanted to say, feeling his touch even through her coat.

'Nothing,' she said, not daring to look at him. She glanced past his shoulder and saw Nita Muller coming from the parking lot on the side of the building. Great, she thought, running into the office eyes and ears was just what I needed.

'Well, good morning, you two,' Nita chirped, her eye on Chase's hand on Darcy's arm, as she hurried past them and into the office building.

Darcy realized in an instant the spin Nita would place on what she saw.

'Marvelous!' She could only hope that the poisontongued receptionist hadn't seen her get out of Chase's car.

Chase followed Darcy's gaze. He frowned. 'Is there something wrong?'

'Everything! Nita is the worst gossip in the office,' she muttered. 'What if she saw us drive up together? What will she think?'

'She'll probably think I gave you a ride to work.'

Darcy stared at him and shook her head. 'I had no idea you were so naive, Mr. Whitaker.' Pulling her arm from his hand, she pushed through the glass doors ahead of him.

Chase relished the sight of her in heels as he followed. The first gift he gave her, he decided, would be a pair of strappy heels two inches taller than the plain pumps she wore. Let her top him by an inch. He didn't care. And a very short dress to go with the shoes, he decided. Any woman with legs like that should show them off.

Perplexed, he kept watching her. Surely she must dress differently away from the office. She had to if Janet was to be believed. Though now that he'd really got to know her, he decided that she didn't need all the trappings women like Claudia wore.

Wow, he could imagine the stir she'd make at the office if she came in wearing a short shirt and high heels. The guys would go nuts! They'd be all over her like hounds after a scent.

Chase frowned. Maybe Darcy should just continue wearing the sober clothes she'd always worn to work. After all, he reasoned, he didn't want her to start a riot.

9

Darcy now believed the old superstition about your ears burning when someone gossiped about you must be true. Hers certainly seemed as if someone had set them on fire.

She saw Nita excitedly chattering on the phone before the door that separated the reception area from the inner offices closed. Now, as she hung up her coat, her face began to burn too, nearly as hot as her ears.

Irritated by Nita's speed to spread gossip, Darcy stalked to her desk and dropped her purse on it. She unlocked her bottom desk drawer and tossed her handbag into it. She sensed Chase behind her. She seemed to have developed radar where he was concerned.

She whirled around. 'Go away,' she hissed.

He held up both hands as if to ward off her ire. His amusement as he complied with her request only fueled her irritation.

Darcy concentrated on unlocking the file cabinets. Then she turned her attention to the work she'd planned for the day. When she saw Janet heading her way, carrying her morning cup of coffee, she scowled, unaccountably angry at her friend.

'Wow! Look at you!' Janet dropped into the chair in front of Darcy's desk. 'Heels and a dress!'

'Do you think it's an improvement?' Darcy snapped.

'It's a start,' Janet replied, sipping from her coffee cup. 'A slow start, but still a start. What prompted it?'

'Oh, nothing,' Darcy said, confused now, when she'd felt so clearheaded in her apartment. Her anger at Janet's interference ebbed. Suddenly, all she felt was a desperate need to confide in her friend — even if her friend was the one who'd started all this.

'Janet, you won't believe what happened last night.' The words tumbled out as she told Janet about the evening, concluding by saying that Chase had kissed her. Kissed her? What a mild way to describe the soul-stirring caresses she and Chase had exchanged.

'He kissed you?' Janet's eyes danced with excitement. She clasped her hands together and gazed prayerfully at the ceiling. 'Thank you! Thank you!'

'Yes,' Darcy looked away from her friend, 'and he did it again this morning,' she mumbled.

'He did?' Janet jumped up and grabbed Darcy's hands. 'That's wonderful, kiddo.' When Darcy didn't share her enthusiasm, Janet's excitement faded. She sat back down.

'What's wrong? Isn't that what you wanted? For Chase to notice you?'

Darcy tugged at her bun. Her hair seemed too tight today. 'That's not all. I guess you'll be gratified to discover that now he wants to have an affair with me.'

'What?!' Janet shouted.

'Shhh. I don't want the whole world to know.' Darcy looked around anxiously. Several of the men looked up, but they soon went back to their work.

'I told him no, of course.'

'You what?'

'Janet, be quiet!' Darcy looked around again. This time her coworkers took longer to shift their attention back to the papers on their desks.

Janet whispered furiously, 'Darcy, I don't understand you at all. You finally get him to notice you — big time — and you turned him down?'

'This is all your fault, Janet. How could you have told him that I was in love with him?'

'I never!'

'Yes, you did. He said he knew my secret so you had to tell him. That's the only secret I've got.'

'Oh,' Janet shifted uneasily. 'I swear I didn't tell him, Darcy. I'd never betray your confidence.'

'Then why would he say that?'

Janet shrugged. 'I don't know,' she said, her eyes studying her coffee intently. 'So why did you refuse his offer?'

'Because I love him! I don't want some sleazy affair.'

'I hate to break this to you, but he's not going to propose marriage. I thought you knew that.'

'I just don't want to be some kind of one-night stand for him,' Darcy whispered in a strangled voice.

'Oh, Darcy, that might be all you can get. Everybody knows he's having an affair with Jack Longvale's daughter.'

'What! Well, if that's true, I won't play musical beds, hoping he lands in mine occasionally!' Darcy whispered furiously. With a guilty start, she then asked, 'Surely he wouldn't come on to me if he were involved with someone else? Would he?'

Janet hooted. 'Wow, are you innocent! Men do it all the time. So do a lot of women nowadays.'

'Well, I don't do that. And I won't. I just don't think that way. If he is involved with Claudia Longvale, I don't want to be the one to come between them.'

'For God's sake, Darcy, he's not married to Claudia. And she's as much a swinger as he is!'

'That doesn't make any difference to me. If I can't have all of him, then I don't want any part of him.'

Janet shook her head in disgust. 'I hate to tell you this, kiddo, but you are seriously behind the times.' She rolled her eyes. 'And after all I did to get him to notice you.'

Darcy stared at her. 'What do you mean, all you did? I thought you said you didn't tell him my secret.'

Janet clapped her hand over her mouth. 'Oh, nothing. I'm just running off at the mouth again.' She leaped out of the chair. 'I didn't tell him. I've got to go now.'

Darcy grabbed Janet's arm and forced the woman to stay. She looked at her squirming friend. 'No, you did something, didn't you?' Suddenly, it made sense. 'You sent those flowers!'

Janet tried to pull away. 'I need to get moving. I've got business out of the office.'

'You're not going anywhere until you tell me everything.'

Guiltily, Janet frowned. 'Darcy, I'm sorry. I probably shouldn't have interfered, but I thought if Chase was interested enough in you to really see you, that you could build on that. I didn't know he was going to steamroll over you.'

At Darcy's stern look, she hung her head and confessed. 'I kind of made him think you were a femme fatale — remember we sort of decided he only wanted a woman who was like the others he dated?'

Darcy nodded and Janet continued. 'So I — uh — like — faked a phone call that he couldn't help but overhear, and I ordered the flowers and kind of, like, told him you had men following you with their tongues hanging out, and stuff like that. You know, like you were Miss Hot Pants.'

Darcy dropped into her chair. 'So you made him think I was a female counterpart to him.' Darcy remembered every kiss she'd given him, every wanton caress she'd pleasured him — and herself — with. No wonder he thought she was passionate and hot-blooded.

'He must think — !' She broke off, as memories of the night before filled her head. That's why he wanted her! Not because he'd suddenly found her charming and irresistible, but because he thought she'd make a perfect playmate.

'So when he said he knew my secret, he meant he knew I was some kind of sex-crazed playgirl!' Anger stirred to life inside her. 'A man like that probably doesn't know the definition of the word love!'

'I'm sorry. I just wanted him to notice you.' Miserably, Janet wrung her hands. 'I knew you wanted him. I just wanted to give you a chance to get what you wanted.'

Darcy laughed harshly. 'Be careful what you wish for, Janet. Remember that.' She covered her mouth with both hands, afraid her laughter would change to sobs. This was the morning from hell, she decided.

'I do have to leave the office, Darcy. Please forgive me, won't you? Call me tonight at home? Okay?' Darcy nodded but didn't reply.

Automatically, her hands began sorting the equipment invoices that were delivered to her desk first thing each morning. Seething, she resolved to push Chase into a tiny corner of her mind. She picked up the first invoice from the pile but couldn't seem to focus on the numbers. Darcy frowned and reached up to remove her glasses to clean them. When her hand touched her face instead of the plastic frames, she realized why she couldn't see. That scoundrel had her glasses in his coat pocket!

Darcy groaned and laid her head on her folded arms. It was too much. She couldn't allow herself to see him until she had her emotions under control. But she had to have her glasses. If she couldn't concentrate on her work today, she'd fall apart.

'Something wrong, Darcy?' Nita Muller asked sweetly, tapping her inch-long acrylic fingernails on a coffee mug as she passed Darcy's cubicle. 'Want me to get you a cup of coffee, dear?'

Darcy controlled her expression before lifting her head. Nita didn't need to pass her desk to get to the kitchen. The busybody was just looking for grist for her gossip mill. 'Nothing's wrong, Nita. I'll take a raincheck on the coffee,' she replied just as sweetly.

An hour later Darcy surrendered. She'd tried holding the invoices at arm's length but her eyes were burning — from the strain of focusing, she told herself, not from the unshed tears of humiliation that stung her eyes. There was no reason she should be reluctant to face Chase Whitaker, she told herself.

She had nothing to be ashamed of just because of a stupid trick Janet had played. In fact, if she explained it to Chase, he'd understand. Very likely he'd see the humor in thinking that Darcy was desirable and sensuous. He'd probably have a good laugh about it. Then he'd leave her alone. But that was what she wanted, wasn't it?

Darcy squared her shoulders and headed to Chase's office. His door was open, but he was on the phone. He beckoned her to enter and gestured toward a chair.

Darcy pantomimed that she needed her glasses, but he acted as if he didn't understand. Fuming, she paced the room. She knew he understood what she wanted. He was just being difficult.

'Well, John, as soon as your attorney finishes looking over the Pinto Flats agreement, we're ready to sign.' Chase grinned and made a vee for victory sign with his fingers.

He hung up the phone and looked at her, his eyes shining with excitement.

'That was John Tillman.' Then a wide grin spread across his face. 'I did it, Darcy.' He heaved a sigh of relief. 'Pinto Flats is a done deal, just waiting for the signatures. Longvale and Tillman are supposed to sign the papers this week.'

Darcy couldn't help the feeling of happiness that filled her. She forgot for the moment her anger and hurt. Chase had accomplished what so many had said was impossible. He'd brought Sunbelt Oil back from the brink. His company — his baby — would be on top again. She couldn't help feeling proud of him.

'Congratulations, Chase. I'm happy for you. I know what this means for the company. And how much the company means to you.' It was probably the only thing in his life which he truly loved, Darcy thought miserably.

He whooped. Leaping from his chair, he strode to the doorway and called out, 'Looks like the Pinto Flats project is going through. It's almost a done deal.' Loud whoops greeted his words.

Darcy heard the cheers and excited chatter drifting through the offices. She smiled when he turned to her. Her smile faded when she saw the intensity of his blue gaze.

'I'll come back later,' she said, rising.

Chase closed the door and leaned against it. His predatory expression reminded Darcy of some primitive war chief who planned on celebrating victory in a very elemental way. She gulped and stepped back. Chase walked slowly toward her. Her heart began to hammer, making it difficult to breathe properly. She tried to remember that she was angry with him. That he was a scoundrel.

'Why don't you show me how happy you are?' he asked.

'What — what do you mean?' Darcy was pretty sure she knew what he meant. By now, she recognized *that* look in his eyes. But that look was based on a totally false perception on his part. She should tell him so. She would tell him so. But the words wouldn't take shape.

Her body responded to him on some level below conscious thought, swelling, heating. Anticipating. She backed up another step. Her knees caught the arm of the couch, and she lost her balance, falling backwards onto the soft leather.

'Now that's an interesting position,' Chase said with a devilish smile, tracing his index finger along the hem of her dress where it rested against her upper thighs. 'You have the most gorgeous legs,' he added, in a voice as smooth as silk. His eyes slid up her legs like a caress.

When his eyes met hers, Darcy thought something — possibly a volcano inside her — reached the melting point and erupted, burning away all her logic and objections. She felt hot all over, deliciously hot and languid. She couldn't have moved if her life depended on it.

Chase bent and kissed each leg just below the dress hem. Then he came around the couch and sat on the edge, leaning over her. Darcy closed her eyes — prepared for his kiss, longing for it. When his lips met hers, she sighed and her arms rose to encircle his neck, drawing him down to her. Just one more kiss, she reasoned, then she'd tell him how mistaken he was.

A loud knock on the door intruded. Darcy's eyes snapped open.

'Go away,' Chase called.

Shocked at how easily she'd yielded, Darcy jerked, knocking Chase off balance. He slid to the floor, landing on his rear with a loud thump.

The office door flew open. Darcy yanked her legs off the end of the sofa and jackknifed to a sitting position.

'What the hell is going on here?' the man in the doorway angrily demanded, his silver eyes raking her from her disheveled hair to her hiked-up skirt. 'Well?'

All conversation in the outer office halted at the snarled question from the man who towered over them.

'Bruce!' Darcy yelped, leaping to her

145

feet and tugging at her skirt. Of all times for her brother to show up at the office! 'It's not what you think.' She tried to smooth the stray hairs back into her bun, as Chase rose to his feet.

Bruce looked from her to Chase, with an expression that promised retribution for the man who'd dallied with his sister. He snorted. 'I'd say it's exactly what I think.'

Chase scowled and took a step toward Bruce. 'What do you mean just barging in here?'

'Your secretary told me to go right in.' Bruce stalked over and grabbed Darcy's wrist. 'Looks like I was just in time, too.' He pulled on her arm. 'Come on, Stretch. You're leaving.'

Darcy resisted. 'Bruce, I've got work to do.'

Bruce withered her with a look from his silver eyes. 'If that's a sample of the work you do around here, I think you need to find another job.'

'Now just a minute,' Chase began, grabbing Darcy's other arm. 'She's not going anywhere with you. Just who do you think you are?'

'I'm her brother, that's who!'

Darcy felt like a T-bone steak caught between two hungry dogs. Bruce had always been overprotective. Darcy could tell he was just waiting for a chance to tear into Chase. She sighed. Her brothers had always thought they could tomcat around all they wanted, but their little sister had to be as pure as the driven snow.

'Her brother?' Chase clapped Bruce on the back. 'Well, that's different. I thought you were one of her lovers.'

'One of her what?' Darcy and Bruce asked in horrified unison.

Uh-oh, Darcy thought, looking up at her brother. There was going to be hell to pay.

'Okay, Stretch, you have a lot of explaining to do. I'll get back to you, Whitaker,' Bruce said, jabbing his right index finger at Chase.

'I'll be here,' Chase answered, standing his ground.

Darcy sighed and jerked her arms away from both of them. 'You men are so typical. There won't be any confrontation. This is just a misunderstanding.'

Chase grinned at her and said, 'Don't get so upset. Your brother and I aren't going to duke it out over your honor. Run along and visit with him, Stretch,' he added with a grin. When Darcy glared at him, he chuckled.

Despite her assurances, how was she going to explain this to Bruce? And Chase's remark about her lovers? She was beginning to get a headache, she realized, rubbing her forehead. Then she remembered. No wonder her head hurt — Chase still had her glasses.

Bruce grabbed her wrist again and pulled her to the door.

'Quit dragging me around, you big bully. This isn't tug of war.' Darcy jerked her wrist loose and rubbed it. 'I'll be lucky to have any skin left,' she grumbled.

'I'd be more worried about the skin on your throat,' he grumbled. 'I haven't seen hickeys like that since high school.'

10

'What are you doing here anyway?' Darcy asked, her face as red as the velvet bows on the Christmas tree.

She forced him to follow her to the kitchen for a cup of desperately needed coffee. Maybe the jolt of caffeine would bring her to her senses. How could she have let herself get carried away like that? It must have been Chase's exuberance at closing the Pinto Flats deal. That had to be the answer. She was just as excited about it as he was, she reasoned. That's all it was.

'I was worried about you. I came to see how your ankle was.'

Darcy refused to be intimidated by her brother's scowl. He studied her for a moment. 'Apparently, it made a swift recovery.'

'I told you my ankle was all — ,' Darcy began, but Bruce interrupted her, firing one question after another at her before she could even answer the first one.

'Why don't you just work me over with a rubber hose?' she complained.

'Would it do any good? You're more closemouthed than some of the cons I deal with.' He stood and walked over to select a pastry from the bakery carton on the counter. 'If you had nothing to hide, you'd come clean with me.'

'Don't try that policeman psychology on me. I'm not a crook.' Darcy rubbed her forehead tiredly.

Bruce grinned. 'If I remember my American history, didn't President Nixon say that just before he resigned?'

'I know you mean well, Bruce, but I don't need you to manage my life for me. Anyway, you ought to be happy. You're off the hook with Mom.'

'What do you mean?'

'You don't have to fix me up now that you know I have a man interested in me,' she said, her voice just a shade too sweet.

'Don't get sarcastic with me, little sis. Besides, that isn't just some man. He's your boss, you goose. What happens when this affair is over? How will that affect your position here?'

Darcy rolled her eyes. 'I didn't say I was having an affair with him! I just said he was interested in me.' No way was she going to give her big brother more ammunition by confessing that Chase did want to have an affair with her.

'Besides,' she bluffed, 'even if I decided to have an affair, we're both adults. This is the nineties,' she said, trying to sound breezy and nonchalant. 'I don't know how to put this delicately, but I have been around the block.' A very short block, Darcy thought, recalling the one lackluster romance she'd had in college. If you looked up the word boring in the dictionary, you'd be certain to find the picture of her old boyfriend.

'Geez, Darcy! Don't say stuff like that.' Bruce glared at her.

Darcy laughed. 'Bruce, people don't get so possessive anymore about their,' she faltered, falling short of the jaded sophistication she'd strived for, 'Their . . .'

'Lover is the word you're trying to say,' Bruce finished for her with a scowl. 'And that word reminds me of something else I want to ask, but first let me correct your erroneous assumption. I see the results of ruined love affairs every day of the week, and it's not a pretty sight.

'You know that old saying that goes something like, 'Hell hath no fury like a woman scorned'?' he asked. 'Well, you can make that a woman or a man scorned. When you and your boss finish fooling around, you may find yourself looking for another job.'

'That won't happen.' Darcy shook her head emphatically. His dire prediction made her uneasy. She'd been so busy obsessing about the emotional consequences of an affair with the man she'd loved for two long years that she hadn't even thought of the real complications it could cause. She just didn't have enough experience to play this game, she decided.

'I hope for your sake it doesn't.' As Bruce took the last bite of the sweet pastry, his pager beeped. 'Can I use your phone, Stretch?' He stalked off without waiting for permission, leaving his coffee cup and sprinkles of powdered sugar on the table.

'Autocrat,' Darcy muttered, cleaning up after him. She pitied the woman who ended up with her brother. Whoever it was, she'd better like picking up after the big slob.

When she returned to her desk, he was finishing his conversation. A minute later, he pecked her on the cheek and tugged at her collapsing bun. 'Got to run, Stretch, but you and I are going to finish this conversation.' He shook his index finger at her. 'Especially that part about your other lovers. You can bet on it.'

He dashed out the door, and Darcy tried to settle into her work routine.

She didn't want to think about Bruce's warning. She didn't need it because she had no intention of having an affair with Chase.

Then you should quit climbing all over him the minute he touches you, a little voice inside berated.

If only I could, Darcy thought, turning on her computer, but the moment she got near him, her brain shut down. The only thing that worked was her emotions — and her nerve endings. The answer to her quandary was simple. Stay away from him.

Darcy sighed and brushed aside strands of hair that straggled onto her face. She wished she could brush aside her attraction to Chase Whitaker as easily. She poked the loose strands back into her bun, but they kept slipping out. Even her hair was against her today, she thought in irritation, picking up an invoice. She gazed blindly at it.

Darcy wanted to wail. She still couldn't work the darn things because she hadn't yet liberated her glasses from Chase's pocket.

Nita Muller chose that moment to stroll by again. 'Everything all right, Darcy dear?' she called out sweetly.

'Just fine, Nita,' Darcy replied, gritting her teeth. Who had appointed that woman the office monitor? Even though she knew why Nita felt she'd been cheated out of the accounting position, her sympathy had faded during the two years she'd worked with the gossipy receptionist. She picked up an invoice and pretended to study it as she waited for Nita to flounce back to her desk.

Darcy waited for five of the longest minutes in her life, then looked to make sure everyone was tending his or her own business before stalking into Chase's office. She stopped five feet from his desk. She didn't dare close his office door, not trusting him — or herself.

'Your brother leave already?' Chase looked up from some papers he was signing. His grin annoyed her intensely.

'Listen, this has got to stop,' Darcy said in a low voice, trying to make sure no one eavesdropped on her conversation.

'What are you talking about?' Chase stacked the pages neatly and laid down his pen. He leaned back and crossed his hands behind his head as he studied her. How could he have ever thought she was plain? He'd known her for two years, respected her ability, and treasured her loyalty, but he'd been blind to her subtle beauty, deaf to her husky, sexy voice, and oblivious to her sensuality. He looked at her mouth and found himself smiling, remembering the way it felt against his.

The lazy smile he offered her told Darcy that he knew exactly what she was talking about.

'You know perfectly well what I mean.' Darcy glanced over her shoulder to see if anyone was watching and met half the eyes in the outer office.

Chase followed her gaze. 'Why don't

we discuss this more privately?' he suggested softly. 'Close the door.'

'Oh, no. You're just plain crazy if you think I'm going to closet myself in here with you again.'

'Not afraid, are you?' he teased.

'Of course not.' Darcy thrust her chin out defiantly. 'I just don't want the whole office speculating on what we're doing in here.'

'Well, if it hadn't been for your brother, no one would think we were doing anything other than discussing business — just like we've done every day for the past two years.' His chair creaked as he leaned back. 'If you won't close the door, then go to lunch with me. We'll discuss this flaming affair that we're not having. Yet.'

'We're not having it ever,' Darcy declared.

His hot eyes devoured her from the top of her head to her toes. Darcy tingled, especially in parts of her anatomy she was glad were hidden from his view. 'Don't look at me like that!'

'Like what?' he asked innocently, his eyes dropping to her chest.

Darcy groaned and refrained from crossing her arms in front of her chest. 'Just tell me where you want to go, and I'll meet you,' she said between gritted teeth.

'Your gracious acceptance of my lunch invitation overwhelms me,' he teased, seemingly unperturbed.

'Tough,' she said. 'So where do I meet you?'

'Tsk tsk tsk,' he chided gently. 'You'll have to go with me, Darcy. You don't have a car. Remember?' He rocked back in his chair.

'I'm not walking out of here, hand in hand with you, so everyone can wonder where we're going and what we're going to do when we get there!'

'Hmmm. I can think of several places we could go and several rather spectacular things we could do.' When she looked aghast, Chase held his hands up in surrender. He laughed. 'Okay, if you insist on maintaining this facade of primness then I guess we'll have to sneak around. Take my keys. Leave the office a little early, and wait for me in the car. You can even hide under the blanket on the backseat if it'll make you feel better.'

He stood and fished his keys out of his pocket. 'Do you want me to toss them to you or can you risk getting close enough for me to hand them to you?' he asked archly.

Darcy's look would have frozen the water that flowed through San Antonio's River Walk — even in July. With a scowl, she walked over and grabbed his keys. 'You have a ridiculously silly grin on your face,' she declared with great dignity, but her words only served to increase his amusement.

Darcy stomped back to her cubicle. She couldn't concentrate on anything but the hands on the clock as the minutes that dragged by. Finally, at eleven forty-five, she couldn't take the strain any longer.

Chase was walking out of his office as

she pulled on her coat. Great timing, Darcy, she scolded herself as she walked past him. When she pushed through the double doors, the icy wind slapped her in the face, taking her breath away, and cooling her flaming face.

She hurried to his car. When she slid onto the leather seat she shivered. It was like sitting on an ice floe in the Arctic.

A few minutes later she saw Chase run from the office, unbuttoned over-coat flapping in the breeze. Despite everything, she found herself marveling at his physical appeal.

He jumped into the driver's seat. 'What's the matter? Cold?' He reached for her. His arms wrapped around her before she knew what was happening.

He was so warm, and he smelled so good. She closed her eyes and sighed, unconsciously snuggling into his arms as if it were the most natural thing in the world to do.

Then, to her consternation, he kissed

her! Immediately, all her resolutions and vows vanished. She kissed him back. One kiss led to another. She reached inside his coat, her hands sliding up his chest and curling around his neck.

A car horn from the street blasted her back to earth.

'Oh, no!' She pushed away from him. 'Quit it, Chase!'

'I will if you will.' Laughing, he started the engine. 'We are definitely going to have a long talk,' he said, pulling out of the parking lot with a squeal of tires.

'Where are we going?' Darcy asked stiffly, after they'd passed several nearby restaurants.

'The Mission Hotel on the River Walk,' he said.

'What? You can forget it. I'm not going to bed with you!'

11

Chase slanted a look at Darcy. 'So you say. Quite frequently, as a matter of fact. You must be spending a lot of time thinking about doing just that since you bring it up so often.'

Darcy clamped her lips together. She wasn't going to say another word!

They rode along in silence for a few minutes. 'What's the matter? Cat got your tongue?' Chase prodded.

Darcy deigned to look at him. 'I think we can finish our talk over lunch, if that is indeed what you have in mind,' she replied primly.

He kept his eyes on the fast-paced noonday traffic. A smile hovered on his lips. He loved it when she sounded so proper and correct. Especially when he had found out what she was really like. It was like knowing a secret that no one else knew. A moment later he said huskily, 'Don't pout, Désirée.'

Darcy scowled. 'I told you not to call me that.'

'It's a pretty name. I like it. Your mother must have liked it or she wouldn't have named you that.'

Darcy frowned. 'You don't know my mother.'

'Why did she name you Désirée?'

'For the same reason she named me Darcy.'

'That's enlightening.' He laughed. 'Come on, don't sulk. Tell me.'

Darcy gazed at Chase's profile. Why couldn't he be ugly, with a hooked nose, and beady eyes? 'Why do you want to know?'

'Because I want to know all about you. Every detail. Until yesterday, I thought I knew everything — like, you're smart, loyal, faithful, and honest.'

'You make me sound like a basset hound,' Darcy grumbled.

He grinned. 'I know all kinds of things about you as an employee, but I don't know anything about you as a woman — except that you're extremely passionate. You're quite an enigma, Darcy Désirée Benton.'

After she told him about Janet's trick, he'd realize the boring Darcy Benton he'd known all along was the real woman. She knew he wouldn't want anything to do with her after that. The thought depressed her immensely. What harm would it do to delay the moment of truth? For a little while longer, she wanted to pretend that she was the woman created by his imagination from Janet's fibs.

'So tell me about your name.'

'You really want to know?' When he nodded, she continued, 'My mother is Cajun French from Louisiana. When she married my dad, who's a transplanted Yankee, she wanted to keep her French heritage alive so she gave each of us kids names that had French origins.'

'I didn't know Darcy was a French name.'

Darcy wrinkled her nose. 'It means

dark fortress, which of course gave my brothers a reason to call me Fort Darcy, among other things.'

'Like Stretch?' Chase grinned.

She nodded, relaxing as she talked about her family. 'Bruce, Marc, and Royce, my brothers, all hated their names, but Dad kept telling them it could have been worse. They could have been Beauregard, Maurice, and Raoul.'

Chase whooped with laughter. 'Just wait till I see Beauregard again.'

Darcy's grin was unrepentant. 'I called them those names whenever they started in on me. And you can imagine how often I got picked on since I was the baby girl of the family.'

'What does Désirée mean?'

'Oh, that's just from that old movie about Napoleon and the woman who was supposed to be his first love. Did you ever see it? Marlon Brando played Napoleon, and Jean Simmons, I think, played Désirée. My mom loved that movie.'

Chase parked the Cadillac and cut the engine. 'But what does it mean?' he asked, reaching out to lay a hand on her shoulder.

Darcy moistened her lips. 'Longed for,' she whispered. She felt his hand move to her head, and the next minute her hair cascaded down. 'What are you doing?'

'Something I've longed for,' he said, threading his hands through her hair.

She reached up, searching for the hairpins, but he held them in his hand. 'Give me those!'

'I'll give them to you before we get back to the office.' He dropped the pins in the same pocket that held her glasses and patted the pocket. 'I want to see your hair loose and free.'

Darcy hated it when his voice dropped to that meet-me-in-the-bedroom tone. At least she wanted to hate it, she thought.

He moved closer and ran his hands through the length of her hair, gently pulling the strands into a semblance of order. 'There,' he said, arranging her hair about her shoulders.

Darcy noticed his breathing was as uneven as hers. Her mouth seemed suddenly as dry as the west Texas dust. She cleared her throat and looked away from his searing gaze. 'We should go in.' She looked at the entrance to the luxury hotel. Safety lay within its doors.

'I guess we should,' he sighed, wrapping his hand in a long silky lock of hair. 'You have the most beautiful hair.' Slowly he drew the strand through his fingers.

Darcy stared at him in surprise. 'Thank you,' she murmured.

He looked into her eyes, and she felt herself softening toward him for just a moment. Then he opened the door, stepped out and hurried around to open her door.

Darcy took a deep breath of the bracing air, knowing she'd need her wits about her while in his presence. So far she was batting a thousand on the wimp team.

Once seated in the restaurant, they

were waited on immediately. Darcy couldn't even pretend to be hungry but she ordered a sandwich anyway.

'Now, let's talk about this passionate affair we're going to have,' Chase said, reaching for her hand and clasping it in his.

'You mean the one we are *not* going to have,' Darcy said.

'Now that's where we disagree. I think it's just a matter of time before you accept the inevitable. You may have had some silly rule about not getting involved with men at work, but last night changed all that. We're already involved.' His thumb caressed the soft skin between her thumb and index finger.

Darcy stared at the tiny bit of skin he stroked, marveling that he could elicit such a highly charged response from a few millimeters of skin.

'I'm willing to bet that you can't stop thinking about last night either, Darcy. About how it felt to be in my arms, with my hands on your body, and your hands on mine.'

'Don't say those things!' Darcy pleaded. 'I want you to stop talking like that. And stop kissing me and touching me and looking at me like that!'

'Like what?' he asked innocently.

'Like you're looking right now! As if you're imagining what it would feel like to — ' Darcy shut her mouth abruptly, aware that she'd almost said what she had been thinking.

His eyes blazed. 'To what, Darcy? To hold you with no barrier of clothes between us? To sink into your warmth? To see if we could defy the laws of physics and make the earth move?'

Stricken, Darcy could only nod, abashed at her breathless response to his mesmerizing voice. If only she didn't yearn so badly to feel those things. With him.

He didn't love her, she reminded herself. He just wanted her. No, he didn't even want her, she thought miserably. He wanted some mythical woman — the femme fatale — that

Janet had described. And she wasn't anything like that. As bad as she hated to, she had to tell him the truth.

'I guess I can understand why you think you want to . . . to sleep with me, but you don't really want to, Chase!'

'I don't?' Chase asked, bemused. 'What makes you say that?' He lifted his other hand and stroked her cheek. Without giving her a chance to answer, he continued, 'Don't fight it so hard, Désirée. I can make you forget your other lovers. Give me a chance, and I'll prove it to you.'

'That's just it,' Darcy cried, 'there aren't — '

Their waiter chose that moment to deliver their lunch. Though it was artfully arranged, even a work of art as far as chicken salad sandwiches go, Darcy couldn't eat a bite.

'I need to tell you — '

'Chase, darling!'

Darcy groaned in despair. What was Claudia Longvale doing here?

'I didn't know you were going to be

lunching here today!' the beautiful blonde exclaimed.

Chase dropped Darcy's hand — like a hot potato, she thought resentfully. He stood, offering his hand politely to the woman. She clasped it in both her hands, hugging it to her voluptuous breasts and standing on tiptoe to press a kiss to his cheek. The kiss left a scarlet lip print on his face.

Darcy wanted to shove the woman away — far away — like to the state of Alaska maybe. Her hand still lay on top of the table where Chase had been teasing and fondling it. She looked at it as if it were an abandoned lover.

Darcy folded both her hands in her lap and watched the other woman work. Claudia could have written an instruction manual on being a femme fatale. She should have looked laughable in the tight red leather microskirt and jacket, but she didn't. She looked sexy and chic. Even the red leather gloves looked perfect with the expensive outfit. Anyone else wearing such a get-up would probably be arrested by the fashion police.

Chase introduced Darcy, but Claudia had eyes only for Chase. She wasted none of her considerable charm on Darcy.

Claudia Longvale was the perfect example of the kind of woman Chase desired. Not that Darcy needed a reminder. Nervously, Darcy smoothed her hair. With her features frozen into a mask of politeness, she listened to the animated conversation the woman carried on with Chase.

With each smile Claudia directed at Chase, each soft exchange meant for his ears only, Darcy died a little. She felt foolish for wanting to confide to Chase that she wasn't like Claudia. Heavens! He had eyes. He could see that even if he'd been blind.

'My goodness, but you're pale, Miss Benton. It *is* miss, isn't it?' The blonde smiled much too sweetly, Darcy thought.

'Yes, it is. I'm always pale,' she said.

'It's an occupational hazard for accountants.'

'Oh, so that's what you are — a bean counter!' Laughter trilled from her perfectly lipsticked mouth. 'My goodness, you accountants are practically as bad as lawyers.' Then, as if she realized she'd insulted Darcy, she said, 'Oh, no offense intended, my dear.' Claudia Longvale's smile didn't reach her perfect china blue eyes.

'None taken,' Darcy muttered. Not caring if it was rude, she attacked her sandwich to keep from wrapping her hands around the woman's lovely tanned throat.

Still standing, Chase said, 'Would you like to join us?'

Darcy dropped her sandwich on her plate. At least she wouldn't have to worry about being seduced at the table, she thought.

Claudia graced him with a radiant smile and a throaty, 'Thank you, darling.' She sat gracefully in the chair and placed her beautifully manicured hand on his forearm and squeezed. 'I wanted to see you today anyway,' she said.

'Then you should come to my office later,' he replied, picking up his fork to finish his chicken enchilada.

Claudia monopolized Chase in a conversation about people Darcy didn't know except through the society page and gossip column in the newspaper. Her temper flared each time Claudia touched Chase, and the woman found lots of excuses to touch him. Why didn't he tell her to keep her hands to herself?

'Daddy told me the good news about Tillman finally agreeing to all the terms for the Pinto Flats project,' Claudia babbled.

Resentfully, Darcy listened to the woman discuss Chase's company. Apparently, Claudia was smart enough to realize that Sunbelt Oil was the most important thing in Chase's life. So the blonde beauty even had brains, Darcy thought, really depressed now.

How could she possibly compete with all that?

12

Chase wished Darcy would say something. He glanced at her again. A dime probably couldn't be squeezed between her and the passenger door. Ever since Claudia's appearance, she hadn't said ten words. In fact, she'd withdrawn, as if lost in her own thoughts, but an aura of sadness permeated her silence.

He felt a fierce surge of some nameless emotion that made him want to make her smile, to laugh. Even to scold him primly for his lecherous thoughts. 'Are you warm enough?'

'Yes,' she replied softly. Her eyes remained fixed on the road ahead.

'Sorry that Claudia intruded on our lunch.'

'That's all right. I understand how things are,' she hesitated, 'between you.'

'What do you mean?'

Darcy swallowed. 'Everyone in the

175

office knows that you and Claudia are — '

'Are what?' Chase pressed, frowning.

'Lovers,' she said softly.

'Then everyone is wrong.'

For the first time, she looked up. 'Are you saying that you're not involved with her?'

Chase pulled in to the parking lot at a taco stand. He wanted Darcy to understand. Right now, it seemed the most important thing in the world that she realize that he wasn't involved with anyone else.

'Claudia and I are not, and never have been lovers.'

'But Janet said — '

'Hasn't your mother ever told you not to listen to gossip?' Chase softly chided. He reached over and grasped her chin, turning her face until she was forced to look at him.

'Janet may be my oldest friend but she doesn't know every detail of my life. Darcy, I want to make love with you. If I were involved with another woman, I wouldn't be saying that. I'm not the kind of guy who notches my bedpost.'

'But, Janet has told me about some of your — uh — exploits.'

'That was more years ago than I care to remember. I don't know of a guy who doesn't sow a few wild oats when he's fresh out of college.' He shrugged. 'The truth is, I haven't had a relationship with a woman for a long time.'

Darcy was stunned by his confession. 'Honestly?'

'Honestly.'

'And you aren't in love with Claudia?'

He grimaced. 'No, I'm not. I do not know her in the Biblical sense and want to remain unacquainted that way.'

Darcy tried to tell herself that what she felt was relief for Chase's sake. Claudia Longvale just wasn't the kind of woman he should be paired with. He deserved better.

'If that's settled, let's talk about us.'

Darcy stiffened and pulled away. He

swore softly under his breath. 'Now what's the matter?'

'There is no us,' she said quietly, wishing she had the guts to just tell him the truth. But she had just enough feminine pride not to want to appear to be a total loser.

'Well, there can be.' He jerked the car into gear and pulled out of the parking lot. 'Your brother sure as hell thinks there is an us.'

Darcy groaned. 'Don't mention him. If you only knew the trouble you caused this morning. Bruce is going to be a royal pain about this whole matter.'

'I guess brothers take a dim view of a sister having affairs.'

'Dim view? You don't know how lucky you are. When Bruce found us together on the couch, like that, he could have ripped you apart with one hand tied behind his back.'

'I'm no ninety-pound weakling. I think he'd have had to use at least both hands,' Chase said grimly. 'What is he? Some kind of black belt?'

'Yes. In aikido.'

Chase groaned 'Oh, no. Are you serious? Is he an instructor?'

'No, he's a cop — homicide.'

'Now I know I'm in trouble. He's a martial arts expert and a cop?'

Darcy couldn't help but laugh at his stunned expression. 'Take it easy. He isn't going to work you over in a dark alley. He's nice guy.'

'You could have fooled me.'

'I'll talk to him and convince him that what he saw was just a misunderstanding.'

'You'd lie for me?' Chase turned into the Sunbelt Oil parking lot and cut the engine.

'I wouldn't be lying. All we've done is kiss.'

'I know, and it's driving me crazy.' His hand reached out and stroked her jawline.

Darcy flinched. 'Don't do that!' she whispered.

'Why not?'

'What if someone sees?' she asked,

thinking of her conversation with Bruce.

'So someone sees. We're not doing anything shameful.'

'Spoken just like a man.'

'Maybe that's because I am a man.' He grinned.

'If you're a man, people laugh and joke because you've made another conquest. But a woman has to put up with sly looks, innuendoes, and gossip.'

Maybe she could get him to leave her alone without bruising her fragile ego.

Inspired, she said, 'If I sleep with you, then my life will be unbearable,' she concluded, somewhat melodramatically.

'Aren't you exaggerating a little bit?'

Her tousled hair danced around her face as she vehemently shook her head. 'No! I love my job here. I can't bear the thought of being gossiped about and snickered at. And that's what always happens to women who get involved with the boss.'

Chase hadn't considered that, but

she was right. He'd heard too many guys bragging about their corporate conquests — mergers of the sexual kind — to think she was exaggerating.

'Okay, okay. Settle down. I'll figure something out.' He stroked her hand thoughtfully. 'We'll just have to be discreet.'

'How can I be discreet? I can't behave calmly when you touch me,' she said, too honest in her desperation to make him leave her alone.

What was it going to take? For her to confess that she loved him and wanted to marry him, not merely have an affair with him? If all else failed, she could try that. According to that woman comedienne, he'd leave tire marks in his haste to leave.

'Yeah, I kind of feel like I'm stumbling around in a daze, too. But that's preferable to not touching you,' he said, ruefully. Chase thought about what he'd just said. What had happened to him since yesterday? His hands stilled.

He remembered the pile of reports cascading from Darcy's hands yesterday. 'Is that why you have those adorable little accidents when you're around me?'

Darcy wanted to hide. Mortified by his insight, her face flamed. *Adorable?* Hardly.

'It is!' he grinned. 'There's a direct relation between your accidents and me. Now that I think about it, I don't ever recall anything happening around others. In fact, you're damned graceful. Except sometimes — like when I'm around.'

He wondered if her other lovers had that effect on her. He preferred to think he was unique in that respect.

Darcy's crimson face was all the answer he needed.

'Sweet, sensuous Désirée. I'm incredibly dense.' Chase felt humbled by his newfound knowledge. So she did want him! In fact, she'd been aware of him long before he'd returned the favor.

'I apologize for not recognizing all

those charming little goofs for what they were. You didn't have to repress all those seething emotions. We could have been enjoying each other long before now.'

His thumb raked across the knuckles of her right hand, then lazily made circles around each knuckle, before stroking down the length of her fingers.

Darcy jerked her hand from his grasp and tried to brazen it out. 'Enjoying each other? I don't think so.'

'I know so. Why are you fighting it so hard?'

'Just because I'm attracted to you doesn't mean I'm going to sleep with you.' The words were out of her mouth before she could stop them. 'Ohh! Just take no for an answer.' Darcy grabbed for the door handle.

'Don't you want your hairpins?' Chase asked.

She stopped in mid-flight. 'Yes!' She held out her hand. 'And my glasses!'

Chase gave her the pins. He held her glasses out, but didn't immediately release them when she grabbed them.

'Let me know when you're ready to leave work. I'll take you to pick up your car,' he said.

She nodded and nearly ripped her glasses from his hands. She looked back at him and snapped, 'You've got Claudia's lipstick on your face!'

13

Darcy dashed to the double doors and rushed in. She tried to ignore the curious glances that landed on her. Everyone in the office — probably everyone in the entire city, she thought in disgust — knew that she'd gone to lunch with Chase.

She stormed back to her desk and launched herself into her work with a vengeance. She'd get that man and her irrational attraction to him out of her head one way or another, she thought, making red slashes on some accounting worksheets one of the clerks had turned in for review.

Later that afternoon, Chase sauntered by her desk. He dropped a tiny square of white paper onto its cluttered surface. Darcy's heart beat so loudly she was sure everyone in the room could hear it. Carefully she unfolded the note, and read it.

Your place. Tonight at ten.

He called this discreet? She dropped the bit of paper on her desk as if it had singed her fingers. Then she retrieved it and wadded it up quickly, looking around before tossing it into her center desk drawer.

Darcy forced her thoughts back to the accounting work sheets on her desk. They might as well have been written in Swahili for all the sense they made to her now. She rubbed her tired eyes. The stress of the day combined with the lack of sleep last night made her feel like a refugee in the war between the sexes. All she wanted to do was go home and go to bed — alone.

When her phone rang, she grabbed it and snarled a hello into the receiver.

'Goodness, what's the matter with you?' Janet asked.

'You and your tricks, for starters,' Darcy snapped, wishing she could lay all the blame onto Janet, but she had to accept some responsibility. Janet may have started this, but Darcy had kept it going.

Despite her feeble attempts to tell Chase the truth, she had to be honest with herself. She kept stringing him along because she liked his attention. The thought of explaining how dull and boring she really was made her shudder. Especially after having seen Claudia Longvale in action.

'I guess this isn't a good time to remind you that we were going shopping tonight,' Janet said tentatively.

Darcy was saved. 'Wrong, it's the perfect time. Why don't you pick me up at the office? In fact, pick me up a little before five so I can get my car from the grocery store lot. Then I'll meet you at the mall.'

Replacing the phone, Darcy was relieved that she wouldn't have to ride home with Chase. So she was a coward.

Her musings were interrupted when she glanced at Chase's door, just in time to see Claudia. The woman was snapping her leather gloves against her palm as she barged into Chase's office. The day was on a downhill slide for sure.

Chase was bound to pick Claudia over her, despite what he said. If he knew the truth, he'd leave her alone. So, the bottom line was that she really didn't want that to happen. Darcy sighed. Was it so wrong to play this little charade a bit longer?

* ★ ★

'I want to know how on earth you can prefer that . . . that Amazon secretary to me?' Claudia faced Chase with her hands on her hips.

Chase scowled, his face dark with anger. 'If you are referring to Miss Benton, she is not a secretary. She's an accountant and a damned good one too!'

'Accountant, secretary! What's the difference? You couldn't take your eyes off her at lunch! You hardly paid any attention to me at all!' Claudia paced.

'Claudia, just what is going on here? You're completely off base. You and I are friends, that's all. I never gave you any reason to think our relationship would extend beyond that. So don't come in here acting like I betrayed you or something — '

'Oh, Chase!' She burst into tears and sank onto the couch.

'Stop the waterworks. No theatrics. Just tell me straight why you're carrying on like this.'

Her tears ceased immediately. She pulled a tissue from her bag and blotted her eyes carefully.

'Is it so hard to believe that I may have fallen in love with you?'

'Well, yeah. It is.'

'Maybe I just need you to act as if you're in love with me. For a while. Couldn't you do that?'

'What's this all about? Just tell me the truth.'

Claudia pouted. She dropped onto the couch, crossed her arms, and said, 'I just want to make Victor a little jealous.'

At his incredulous expression, she said, 'Well, he's ignoring me! And I hate it. He needs to be taught a lesson.'

'You're playing a dangerous game, Claudia, and I don't think I want to play it with you.'

'Oh, Chase,' she wailed. 'What harm will it do for people to think we're lovers? Just for a little while?'

Chase remembered the look on Darcy's face. 'More than you know. Go find another patsy.'

'No, you think about it, Chase Whitaker, or you might find your precious company won't be participating the Pinto Flats deal after all.'

Claudia walked out of his office and bumped smack into Darcy, who was leaving the company library next door to Chase's office. The pile of computer printouts were knocked out of Darcy's hands. Claudia glared at her. 'Well, if it isn't Miss Benton.'

She loomed over Darcy who crouched on the floor, picking up papers. 'Did you enjoy your lunch with your boss?'

At Darcy's quiet affirmative, Claudia sneered. 'I just bet you did. I bet that's not all you enjoyed either!' With that parting remark, she whirled and stormed out of the office.

All the blood rushed to Darcy's face. The quiet murmur of conversation in the office died. She hurriedly gathered all the lease papers and computer printouts into a sloppy pile.

'Are you all right?' Angry color suffused Chase's face, but his voice was gentle. 'I'm sorry, Darcy. Sometimes Claudia isn't a very nice person. She's got some whim in her head and won't let it go.'

'I'm fine.' Darcy didn't know what else to say.

Chase dropped to the floor and started gathering papers also. His arm brushed hers. Everything she'd just collected spilled from her hands. Darcy murmured, 'Please, I'll finish this. Just leave me alone.'

She felt as if she were all thumbs as she raked everything into a pile and stood, clutching the mass of papers to her chest. Darcy glanced at Claudia's swiftly retreating back. That woman had the ability to make her feel about as attractive as a slug.

'I have a cure for that little coordination problem we were discussing earlier,' he said softly.

Darcy looked at him and some of the tension went out of her body. Claudia might make her feel ugly, but Chase made her feel as if she were beautiful and desirable. And she adored that feeling. So when he took her arm and led her into his office and closed the door, she didn't resist.

'I feel a little clumsy too,' Chase confessed. 'I want to hold you and kiss you, but I want it so desperately that I'm afraid I might crush you in my eagerness.'

Yes, she thought, that was what she wanted to hear. She leaned against the wall behind her and inhaled his scent as he leaned toward her, bracing himself with his left hand on the wall, nearly touching her body, neatly pinning her in.

Why fight it? She felt the warmth from his body. Her eyelids felt incredibly heavy. Each second that ticked past seemed to last as long as an hour. She thought that she could actually hear the heavy pounding of her heart.

Their eyes met and held. Oh, how she wanted him to kiss her. He smiled as if he knew her thoughts. 'Since I first kissed you last night, you ensnared me. There's no room inside my head for anything except thoughts of you.'

'Shut up and kiss me,' she muttered.

He did.

When they came up for air, he whispered against the side of her throat, 'I want to make love to you, Darcy.'

She hesitated, wanting to tell him yes.

'If nothing else,' Chase said, 'I think you ought to let me make love to you in the interest of science.'

His teasing released her from his seductive spell. She ducked under his arm and walked over to the door.

'Now I've heard everything!' She laughed. 'Explain this creative rationalization, please.'

'I propose a strictly objective, highly scientific experiment.' He grinned mischievously, following her. 'We could see at what point you become coordinated and accident-free around me. It might only take more kissing, possibly some stroking.'

'With or without my clothes?' Darcy asked sarcastically, trying to be as casual as he, despite her soaring pulse rate.

'Oh, definitely without.' He grinned wickedly. 'And if that's not enough, then we could advance to some more advanced stimuli such as nibbling. Bodies rubbing against each other. Intimate, sensitive parts pressing together. I'll do anything to advance the cause of science,' he teased.

Despite the mental images formed by his words and the rush of desire in her body, Darcy found herself smiling at his silliness.

'Then if you still aren't cured, I'm willing to make the ultimate sacrifice and give my poor body to you. Do with it as you will.' He spread both arms as if to offer himself up on the altar of her desire.

Darcy couldn't suppress the laugh that bubbled upward.

'That's better,' he said, reaching for the doorknob. 'I like it when you laugh — when you look happy.'

A pounding on the door sent them springing apart. Claudia Longvale barged in. Did the woman have radar, Darcy wondered?

'Excuse me. I forgot my gloves.' Claudia's icy voice brought Darcy back to earth. Chase rubbed his hand over his face.

Darcy blushed furiously and stammered, 'I need to g-get back to w-work.'

'Oh, do you really work here? What exactly is it that you do for Chase?' Her voice left no doubt as to what she thought Darcy's function might be.

'Claudia, that's enough!' Chase snapped.

The color drained from Darcy's face at the innuendo. With all the dignity she could muster, she said, 'If you'll excuse me, I'll return to my desk.'

'That's a very good idea, Miss Benton. In fact, perhaps you should focus on accounting.'

Chase glared at Claudia. 'Miss Benton knows how to do her job without any instruction from you. I think you'd better leave, Claudia,' he bit out.

'Why, Chase Whitaker! You can't talk to me that way! What do you think Daddy will say when I tell him how rude you were?'

'I don't really give a good — '

Darcy didn't wait to hear the rest of their argument. Mortified by the scene, she excused herself and hurried to the restroom, passing Nita Mullins in the hall. Great! In case someone hadn't witnessed that nasty scene, Nosy Nita would make sure they knew about it before the day's over, she thought.

Darcy began to repair her hairstyle to give herself some time to think. She pulled out the pins and then wound her tresses into a tight bun.

When Nita entered the restroom a few minutes later, Darcy wanted to scream.

'I saw you chatting with Chase's girlfriend,' Nita began, her faded blue eyes peering intently at Darcy.

The hairpins spilled from Darcy's hand, scattering like thistles in a spring wind. She gripped the edge of the sink. They were just friends, she wanted to say.

Nita stroked a brown eyebrow pencil over her toodark penciled brows, accentuating the arch, then pulled back to look at her reflection. 'Don't they make a lovely couple? I'm just holding my breath waiting for the big announcement. Do you think they'll make it at the Christmas party?'

Darcy thought she was going to lose the little bit of lunch she'd managed to swallow.

Chase had told her that he wasn't having an affair with Claudia. She tried hard to believe him. After all, why would he lie? Why indeed?

14

'Janet, if I'd known I'd have to listen to this again, I'd have stayed home.'

'Well, somebody has to talk some sense into you,' Janet said through a mouthful of nachos. 'These are really good,' she said, swiping her mouth with a paper napkin. 'We ought to eat here more often.'

Darcy glanced at the steady stream of shoppers in the mall concourse. 'If you like it so much, why don't you eat more and talk loss?'

'My, my. Aren't we testy tonight.' Janet grinned.

Nothing more was said during the meal, but Darcy sighed when Janet picked up the conversation as they left the food court.

'Janet, please give it a rest. You're treading on thin ice after what you did. You're lucky I'm even speaking to you.

Now I don't want to hear any more about how I'm wasting my life. It *is* my life. I can darn well pine away if I want to.'

Janet raised her hands in mock surrender. 'Okay, if that's the way you want it. But let me say just one last thing.'

Darcy sighed knowing there was no way to stop the outspoken young woman from speaking her mind. Janet might be tiny but she never backed down. 'What is it?'

'For years you've carried this torch for Chase Whitaker. Suddenly, he notices you.' She raised her hands to stop Darcy's outburst. 'I admit I came up with an unconventional method of getting his interest, but you have to admit that he is interested now.'

Darcy started to protest but Janet silenced her with a look.

'So if he's decided to give a real woman a chance instead of those spoiled debutantes he usually dates, what's wrong with taking advantage of that fact?'

'What do you mean?' Darcy asked.

'Granted you're not some playgirl, but he doesn't know that. If his ignorance will give you a shot at winning him, then go for the gold!'

Janet's words tumbled over each other as she walked around Darcy gesturing with her expressive small hands. 'Get rid of that bun. Buy some new clothes. Quit hiding behind those glasses. And don't — definitely don't — tell him that you're just a plain, shy girl without a pack of lovers. Take the initiative. Be the femme fatale. Go to the Christmas party — with or without him.'

'I can't build a relationship on a false premise. I'm not the person he thinks I am.'

Janet snorted. 'It doesn't seem to have stopped him. This might be your chance, Darcy — your only chance — to get the man you love.'

Darcy sighed. 'Oh, Janet, he doesn't want my love. He just wants my body.'

'But that's terrific!'

'What's so terrific about that? I'm not going to have an affair with him.' Darcy crossed her arms stubbornly.

'Darcy, keep telling him no, and you might have a shot at being Mrs. Chase Whitaker. I know Chase. Nothing gets him going like trying to reach a goal. Whatever you do, don't give in to him. Play hard to get, Darcy. Let him chase you, no pun intended, until you catch him!' Janet crowed in delight.

Darcy rolled her eyes and listened to Janet rattle off more advice on how to ensnare Chase before she concluded with, 'Hey, it's worked for hundreds of years. Keep him hot and bothered but whatever you do, don't go to bed with him.

'Now the first thing we have to do is get you some new clothes.' Janet studied Darcy from every angle. 'We'll leave your hair alone, but you have to start wearing it down. And we'll get your face made up so you can see how to apply makeup. The malls close at ten so let's get a move on.'

'Now wait a minute, my petite Chinese friend,' Darcy began.

'No, you listen to me, my tall Caucasian friend. You're going to do this. I know everything you need.'

Darcy listened with horror to the list that included everything from sexy lingerie to electric hair curlers. She had a feeling that she would regret this, but she decided to go along.

★   ★   ★

A few hours later Darcy's feet had suffered as much as her bank balance. Groaning, she dropped onto a bench while she waited for Janet to come out of a store that featured anorexic mannequins dressed in lycra and leather thonglike things.

The dwindling crowd surged around the pine bench like a stream flowing around a rock. What I wouldn't give for a hot relaxing bath and a cup of steaming hot cocoa, Darcy thought wearily. Somebody to rub my aching

203

feet would be nice, too.

'Well, well, well. If it isn't the rather large Miss Benton.' The sarcastic voice came from the doorway of the lingerie shop, opposite the bench where Darcy sat.

Darcy's heart sank. What was Claudia Longvale doing? Making a career of stalking her?

Darcy stood and for the first time in her life, she took perverse pleasure in towering over someone. The blonde had to crane her neck to glare at Darcy.

'Hello, Miss Longvale. How are you?'

'Very well, thank you. Just picking up some last-minute Christmas presents. Do you think Chase will like this?' She slipped a sheer black teddy from the bag.

'It looks a little small for him,' Darcy answered, determined not to get upset. Chase had promised that he wasn't involved with Claudia. But a little voice inside whispered that she was a naive, gullible twit.

Claudia smirked. 'I think he'll like

the fit just fine. He just loves black lace.'

Darcy's stomach burned. She swallowed hard. A mental picture of Claudia overflowing the bodice of the skimpy black silk, materialized in her mind. Her fragile ego began to slip. Then her rebellious imagination cast Chase into the scene. Chase with his large hands stroking the other woman's voluptuous curves.

'If you'll excuse me,' Darcy mumbled, gathering her packages. She felt like a fool for believing that Chase could prefer her to Claudia.

'Oh, don't rush away. Did I embarrass you?' Claudia patted her perfectly styled hair. 'Well, ta ta. I'm off.'

Each word speared Darcy's heart. I'm an idiot, she thought. How could I think he wanted me? Darcy located Janet and suggested they leave.

'Not yet. We haven't got you an evening gown yet.'

'I don't need one, Janet. Why waste the money?' Darcy asked miserably.

'Believe me, it won't be a waste. Just come with me next door. There's a wine red velvet number there that has your name written all over it.'

Resigned, Darcy followed her friend to the expensive boutique. Anything to get this over with. When she saw the floor-length dress with its tight fitted bodice, low scoop neckline and long sleeves, she had to admit that Janet had good taste. Darcy fingered the lush fabric. 'It's beautiful,' she admitted.

Not knowing why she bothered, Darcy headed to the dressing room. Janet followed. A few minutes later, Janet gasped, 'Oh, Darcy, it's you!' The dress, unadorned by fussy beading or lace, fit perfectly. The classic style suited Darcy perfectly, and the wine red made her skin glow.

Darcy had to admit that she'd never worn anything quite so beautiful before. Defiantly, she said, 'I'll take it.' She paid for it and they left, rushing through the freezing rain to their cars.

In parting, Janet said, 'Wear the red wool tomorrow.'

* * *

Darcy parked at her complex and gathered her purchases into her arms, trying to stack everything so she wouldn't have to make another trip down. She stepped backwards and slammed the hatch of the car and bumped into a solid wall of muscle.

A frisson of fear coursed through her and she whirled, sending the small boxes on top flying off into the night.

'Oh, Chase, it's you.' Darcy's eyes closed in relief. 'You scared me to death.'

'Good. You should know better than to have your arms so full when entering your apartment at night. What if I'd been looking for a victim?'

'I don't think most attackers pick on women my size,' Darcy replied dryly. 'And if they did, they'd be sorry. I grew up with three brothers and can give as good as I get.'

'What if he were armed?'

She could see his angry scowl easily in the cold glare of the mercury vapor security lights. 'You're right,' she said, too tired to argue. 'I'm sorry. I'm usually more careful.'

'I'm glad to hear it.'

'Oh, dear.' Darcy looked on the ground. 'Can you get those packages that fell?'

'Sure.' Chase retrieved them from the puddle. The wind blew the water dripping from the bottom of the bags onto his trousers. 'Hope there's nothing that'll ruin in here.' He grabbed a few more packages from the stack she balanced and took her keys from her hand. 'Looks like you did all your Christmas shopping tonight,' he said, leading the way to her front door.

Darcy sighed, too tired to fight him. 'Actually, it's all for me.' Darcy rushed into her apartment, setting the pile of boxes and bags down and turning on lights as she went. 'I decided I needed some new clothes and, uh, some other things.'

Chase put the wet packages on the kitchen counter and turned to her. 'You're late. I was beginning to think you weren't coming home tonight.'

'Why are you here, Chase?' Darcy asked quietly, remembering Claudia's taunts.

'I told you I'd meet you here at ten. Let's not play games anymore, Darcy. You want me. I want you. It's that simple.'

'No, you don't want me. You're just confused,' she mumbled.

Chase walked over to her and lifted her hand to his mouth, planting a kiss in the palm. Then he took her hand and before she knew what he was doing, pressed it against the front of his trousers. 'Does that feel like I'm confused?'

Darcy snatched her hand away as if he'd burned her. 'I told you before that I won't have an affair with you,' she reminded him, her voice shaky.

'Too late, sweetheart. We're already having one, and you can't change your mind now.'

Darcy's heart slammed against her ribs. 'You're not serious.' She forced a laugh.

'Oh, but I am. I've thought about it all evening. I know you want me . . . so don't pretend you don't.'

'Yes. I mean no.' Darcy shook her head. 'I don't know what I mean. You've got me so confused. A few days ago my life was simple and uncomplicated. Now everything is so messed up I don't know what to think.'

'Then quit thinking, Darcy. You think too much.' Chase's hands roved over her back. 'Just feel,' he commanded softly before his lips touched hers.

Darcy's eyes closed and she gave herself to his kiss, drowning in the spiraling desire he always created in her.

'Too much thinking isn't good,' Chase whispered against her lips. His hands moved restlessly over her body, spreading heat wherever they touched. 'Don't deny me, Darcy. Yield to me.'

Almost unbearable heat consumed Darcy. She burned with pure desire, knowing she'd perish if she couldn't feel his skin next to hers.

'Surrender to me,' he murmured. 'Surrender everything.'

The words soaked into Darcy's conscious and her subconscious. Just once, she told herself. The time would come soon enough when he realized she wasn't the woman he thought she was. Then he'd drop her.

Just one night to lie in his arms, she bargained with her conscience. 'I surrender,' she whispered.

15

Why was somebody hammering at this time of the morning? Darcy stretched lazily, wincing at the unexpected soreness in her muscles. Though she burrowed into the pillow, she couldn't block out the noise. One eye opened. She felt confused. Her brain felt fuzzy. She raised her head to listen. That wasn't hammering. That was someone pounding on her door.

Her eyes sought the digital clock on the bedside table. She groaned. She'd overslept. Seven o'clock. Time to get ready for work. First she'd better see what maniac was trying to demolish her door.

Groggy, she sat up and flung the covers aside. Realization hit her like a bucket of ice water. She didn't have a stitch on. The last vestiges of sleep fled. She looked at the pillow next to hers. It hadn't been a dream. Memories of the enchanted night she'd spent in Chase's arms flooded back.

He was still asleep. She wasn't surprised. She didn't imagine they'd had more than a couple of hours of sleep. Her face flamed. Thank goodness the knocking at the door hadn't woken him.

The pounding came again. This time accompanied by the sound of her name being called. Oh, no! It sounded like Bruce.

Darcy dashed to the closet and grabbed her heavy red terrycloth robe. She cinched it tightly and hurried out, making sure to close the bedroom door after her.

With a groan, she saw through the security lens that her worst fears were realized. It was her brother. She snatched the door open and whispered impatiently, 'Stop pounding on my door!'

'Well, let me in. It's cold out here!' He pushed past her, tiny ice pellets

213

dropping from his coat to the carpet.

'What do you want?' she whispered.

'Why are you whispering?' he asked loudly.

'I don't want to wake the neighbors,' she hastily replied.

His head cocked to the side, silver eyes studying her from the tousled hair to her bare feet. 'Were you still in bed?'

'Yes!' Darcy whispered with a glare. Then, in a slightly louder voice, she said again, 'I mean, yes.'

Bruce frowned, his eyes narrowed. 'Is there someone here?'

Darcy's heart thumped. 'No! Don't be silly. I'm just . . . just trying to be considerate of my neighbors. Especially since you made enough noise to wake the dead!'

'Sorry about that, Stretch, but I was freezing my — ' Bruce broke off as he saw the pile of clothes on the floor. His eyes widened. Slowly he turned to take in her appearance.

Darcy shriveled beneath his stare. There was no mistaking a man's white shirt and her black bra lying on top of it. 'It's not what you think,' she began.

'Sweetheart, I'm getting lonely in this big bed of yours.'

Darcy groaned and covered her face with both hands.

Chase, clad only in his unbuttoned trousers, stood in the doorway to the bedroom. He surveyed the scene and frowned. 'Sorry, I didn't know anyone else was here.'

Bruce's head snapped from Chase's sheepish expression to Darcy's horrified face. His icy silver eyes had her nerve endings sending danger signals to her brain. She swallowed. 'Now, Bruce, don't do anything you'll regret,' she began.

'Oh, I won't regret this one bit,' he said, taking a step toward Chase who immediately tensed for the confrontation.

Darcy leaped to Bruce and caught hold of his arm. 'Wait just a darn minute!'

Bruce tried to shake her off, but she

held on tenaciously. 'Let go of me. I'll teach him not to mess with my sister.'

'Bruce, I'm over twenty-one. I know it's hard for you to accept, but I do have the right to a . . . a sex life! You shouldn't have barged in.'

Bruce looked at her reproachfully. 'I was on a stakeout all night. Just thought I'd stop by and have coffee with you.' His look pleaded with her to understand. 'I don't want you to get hurt! I checked around, and I don't like what I found out about Whitaker here.'

Chase growled, 'You investigated me?' Fists clenched, he took a step toward Bruce.

'Yeah, she doesn't need somebody like you in her life.'

Darcy stepped between the two men. 'Both of you, stop it!' After a moment, Darcy said, 'Now, Bruce, go to the kitchen and make some coffee. And I'd like to speak to you privately, Chase.' The two men glared at each other, daring the other to make the first move. 'Please?'

After a moment, her brother's hands relaxed, and he stepped toward the kitchen. 'Okay,' he called back over his shoulder, 'but I'm only making enough for you and me.'

Darcy gathered the pile of clothes from the floor and tugged on Chase's arm. 'Come on. Let's go to the bedroom.' She pushed him through the doorway and closed and locked the door. For a moment her eyes studied the rumpled bed before she dropped the clothes on it.

Chase lifted her chin and gazed into her eyes. She read the hot message in his blue eyes. His hands stroked her hair and pulled her into his arms. She stood in the protective circle of his arms, inhaling his scent, enjoying the rasp of his morning beard as he gently rubbed his face against hers.

His hands moved restlessly on her back, rubbing in circles, soothing the tense muscles bunched in her neck. 'I'm sorry, Darcy, I'd never have embarrassed you in front of your brother.

'I know,' she sighed, closing her eyes. Last night had been the biggest mistake she'd ever made.

'Coffee's ready, Darcy!' Bruce bellowed through the door.

Darcy jumped and looked at the door.

'If you're not out of there in ten minutes — no, make that five — I'm coming in!' Bruce threatened.

Chase scowled. 'Is he your father or your brother?'

'Right now I'd say he has a misplaced paternal complex,' she said dryly, 'which is downright hypocritical when you know Bruce the way I do.'

Chase quirked a brow in question. Darcy pulled away from him. 'He has a playboy reputation as bad as yours.'

'As mine?' Chase crossed his arms and refused to move.

Darcy pushed at him. 'Yes, as yours. Now you've got to get out of here so I can talk some sense into him!'

Chase snorted. 'My reputation is a lot of nonsense.' He looked longingly at the bed, but she shook her head.

Darcy blushed. She tried to keep her eyes from his body as he pulled his clothes on, but she wanted to memorize every detail. She'd never have the opportunity to repeat last night's glorious lovemaking.

'If you keep looking at me like that, I'll never leave,' he complained huskily.

Darcy looked away. 'Sorry,' she murmured, covering her face with her hands.

'Hey, I didn't say I didn't like it. I just don't think your brother could take it if I began ravishing you at this moment.' He pulled her hands away from her face.

Darcy looked shyly at him. 'I . . . I wanted to tell you that last night was . . . '

'Wonderful? Magnificent? Overwhelming? Magical?' He punctuated each word with a soft kiss on her face. 'Earth-shattering?' he asked with another kiss, unable to lie about how it had affected him.

'Time's up!' Bruce bellowed.

'Go shower.' Chase sighed as Darcy hurried to the bathroom.

'I'm going to thrash him within an inch of his life,' he promised. Then he flung the bedroom door open and stood nose to nose with Bruce. 'That's enough, Benton, you've made Darcy uncomfortable enough!'

'I made her uncomfortable? This is all your fault,' Bruce snarled, following Chase to the kitchen.

Chase poured himself a mug of steaming coffee. 'Thanks for the coffee, Benton. Got any donuts on you?' Chase smothered his grin. For Darcy's sake, he could deal with her overprotective brother.

'Look, what's going on with you and my sister?' Bruce blustered, slamming his coffee mug down.

'I'm sure you know exactly what's going on. As Darcy pointed out, she is an independent woman and old enough to know what she wants.'

Bruce just stared at him. 'And what

happens when you finish toying with her?'

Chase frowned. 'I'm not toying with her.'

'Oh, are you saying you're in love with her? You want to marry her?'

Chase's frown changed to a scowl. After last night, he couldn't imagine being with any other woman. Who could please him as much as Darcy had? But marriage?

'I don't think I need to say anything else to you. Let's leave it at this. I respect Darcy and will continue to do so regardless of how this affair ends.'

'Respect. Yeah, right. I'm sure that's all she feels too!' Bruce dumped his coffee in the sink. 'I'll walk you out, Whitaker,' he said, putting a not-so-gentle hand on Chase's shoulder.

Chase resisted the steely grip for a moment but knew it would upset Darcy if he decked her brother in her kitchen, so he gave in as gracefully as possible.

Darcy opened the bedroom door and stepped into the living room. Gone was the wanton woman in his arms last night. In her place was the Darcy that Chase knew from the office. Her wild mane of hair was demurely twisted in a bun at the back of her neck. The heavy glasses rested on the bridge of her nose, and she wore a navy blue suit and white blouse with a little blue bow tie.

Chase grinned. Let the world think she was Miss Prim and Proper. He knew every inch of the beautiful body beneath the prudish clothes. Even her seeming shyness in refusing to meet his eyes entranced him.

Janet had been way off base in describing Darcy. Maybe she had been wild, but she no longer was. If it wasn't for her passionate nature, he would say Janet had made up the entire thing.

'Whitaker and I are leaving, Stretch.'

Darcy looked troubled. 'Now, Bruce, you're not going to — '

Bruce sighed. 'No, as much as I'd like to, I'm not going to beat him senseless. You watch too many old movies. This isn't the forties, Sis. It's the nineties.'

'So everyone keeps telling me,' Darcy muttered.

* * *

Darcy floated through the rest of the morning, barely conscious of the mountain of work on her desk. She'd pick up a report and find herself staring dreamily into space, not remembering what she'd been about to do. Why pretend she didn't want to be with Chase? Last night had been everything she could have hoped for — no, it had been more than she'd ever imagined.

The phone rang. When she lifted it, she heard Chase ask her to bring the report on the workover rig in Lea County, New Mexico, to him. Smiling, she picked up some papers — she couldn't have said whether they pertained to New Mexico or New York — and hurried to his office.

As she entered, she said, 'Here's that report you needed, Mr. Whitaker.'

Chase grinned at her. 'Good. Close

the door and have a seat.'

Darcy shut the door and turned, bumping into him. Chase lost his balance. Darcy grabbed for him and saved him from falling.

Clutching him, she asked with a giggle, 'Now who's clumsy?'

'What do you suggest as a cure?' he asked, straightening. He deftly removed her glasses and tucked them into his coat pocket.

Darcy's breath hitched. 'Well, there's this theory about clumsiness that I heard.'

Chase nibbled on her lips. 'Yes,' he urged, 'tell me more.'

Darcy laughed softly, 'Well, it's my understanding that a certain amount of kissing,' she pressed a quick kiss to his mouth, moving back before he could deepen the kiss, 'and touching,' her hands slid down toward his waist. His breath caught when she gripped his belt.

'Why, Mr. Whitaker, what is it?'

'You tease!' He laughed and curved

his hands around her bottom. Darcy jumped, sending both of them staggering against the desk and knocking over the lamp. The noise sounded extremely loud in the small room.

Chase sighed mournfully. 'I hadn't realized how confining this room is. I guess I'll just have to wait until later to learn more about this interesting theory. For now, I guess I'll settle for,' he stroked his chin and stared at the ceiling as if in thought, feigning nonchalance, 'a kiss.'

Feeling playful, Darcy backed away. 'No, I don't think that's a good idea.'

'Why not? Just one kiss? One little, bitty kiss? To tide me over until tonight?'

'Tonight?' she asked, breathless with anticipation. She'd have him again tonight, she thought, thrilled at the idea.

He caught her hands and lifted them to his shoulders. For each step he took toward her, she backed up a step until her back was literally against the wall.

Darcy yielded to a pressure greater than her willpower. She'd loved him for so long and after a taste of paradise, it was hard to deny herself another nibble.

16

Darcy smiled a sleepy good morning at Chase — at her lover, she thought.

He smoothed her tangled hair away from her face. 'I'll see you later at the office,' he said, pressing a kiss to her forehead.

He felt as if he'd done this a thousand times before. The feeling overwhelmed him. Nothing had ever felt so completely right before.

He hated to leave but he didn't want to risk embarrassing her again in case her overprotective brother decided to drop by.

He made sure the door locked behind him then sauntered down the stairs, whistling *Jingle Bells* as he stretched his arms over his head. It was still dark outside.

'I thought I might find you here.'

The tune died on his lips. Darcy's

brother stood on the bottom step.

Chase rolled his eyes. 'Isn't there a burglar somewhere or a drug lord you could go chase?'

'Plenty of them. But I think my presence is needed here more. I don't want my sister hurt, Whitaker.' He handed Chase a Styrofoam cup of coffee.

Chase grunted his thanks and pried the lid off the container.

'No offense, but why she had to pick a playboy like you is something I don't understand,' Bruce said, holding up a bag of donuts. 'In case you're hungry.'

Chase laughed. 'Thanks.' He pulled a glazed donut out and bit into the sweet, yeasty confection. 'And for the record, I'm not a playboy. So let's get this over with.'

★　★　★

Darcy went to work at her usual time. She'd swept her hair at the sides and crown into a loose knot, leaving the rest falling in soft waves down her back. A red wool dress cinched at the waist flared softly into a full skirt that just brushed the top of her knees. Matching red pumps encased her feet. Her hands had shaken so hard this morning that she could hardly apply the few cosmetics she'd decided to use. Feeling as if every eye were on her, she removed her coat and hung it on the rack.

About an hour later, she sensed Chase and looked up to see him striding toward her. His eyes widened. 'You look wonderful,' he said, his voice low. He moved closer to her and sniffed. 'What's that perfume?'

'Oh, it's . . . just something I picked up the other night,' she said, trying to sound worldly.

Chase leaned against her desk and crossed one foot over the other. 'What's it called?' A smile accompanied his teasing voice.

Darcy thought he looked so sexy and adorable. She wanted to kiss him, right there in front of everyone. Her face blushed nearly as red as her dress. 'Lover's Kiss,' she whispered.

When he leaned closer to her and delicately sniffed, she saw the pulse throbbing in his throat.

'So that's what a lover's kiss smells like, hmmm?' His eyes caressed her. 'I hope when you went shopping the other night that you bought yourself a dress. Because you're my date for the party tomorrow night. I'll pick you up at eight.'

Before Darcy could answer, her phone rang. Bemused, she answered only to have Nita intrude into her dreamlike state. Carefully she controlled her expression.

'Nita said Miss Longvale is waiting in your office for you.'

'I'll be back,' he said, turning quickly.

Darcy was nonplussed by his haste to get to Claudia. She drummed a pencil on the desktop, curious as to what Claudia had to say today. The woman couldn't seem to stay away. Not that she didn't trust Chase, Darcy thought, grabbing a notepad and hurrying to the library next door to Chase's office. His office door was ajar.

She left the library door open and pulled a property book from the shelf. Sitting at the writing table, she opened the book and pretended to make notes when what she was really trying to do was eavesdrop on the conversation in the next office.

What depths you've sunk to, she scolded herself. But she stayed where she was.

After a bit, she wished she'd remained at her desk. From what she gathered, Claudia was threatening Chase. She intended to have her father withdraw the backing of Longvale Company from the Pinto Flats project. If that happened, Chase would be on the brink of bankruptcy again.

Why? Darcy wondered, hurrying out of the library. Why would Claudia do that?

Around two o'clock, Chase brought some computer printouts to her desk and leaned over her shoulder as if to discuss them. Instead, he murmured huskily, 'Did I tell you how beautiful you looked this morning with your hair tangled and spread all over the pillow?'

Darcy shivered at his husky words. She wanted to ask him about Claudia, but couldn't without divulging that she'd been eavesdropping.

'I wish I could stay around to appreciate you, but I've got to be over at Jack Longvale's office most of the afternoon. I'll call you this evening before I come by.'

Darcy almost floated out of her chair with happiness. She'd see him again tonight. Swiveling her chair around so she could look directly at him, she smiled radiantly. 'Whatever you say, Mr. Whitaker.'

'I'll remember that,' he said with a wink and a slow smile that made her heart pound even harder.

After he walked away, Darcy pursued her work happily, humming along with the Christmas carols on the piped-in music. Every now and then she'd stop and stare into space, planning the evening ahead.

She'd cook for him, she decided. Maybe a pot roast and mashed potatoes. Her brothers said her pot roast was as good as Mom's.

She felt like waltzing around the room. Life was wonderful. Love was wonderful! Maybe happily ever after didn't happen just in fairy tales.

★ ★ ★

By the time she walked into the office the next day, Darcy's rose-colored glasses had cracked. Why hadn't Chase come over last night? He hadn't even called.

Fortunately, since everyone at work was excited about the party tonight, no one paid much attention to her after they'd all commented on her appearance. Their gaiety depressed Darcy even more. They all seemed to have someone. She swallowed through the knot of emotion. She'd thought she had someone. Now she wondered. Surely Chase had a good reason for not calling. But he hadn't come to the office yet today either. Uneasy, Darcy wondered where he was.

After everyone left the office at noon for a nearby restaurant, Darcy breathed a sigh of relief. It hadn't been that difficult fooling her coworkers, but she couldn't bring herself to join them in the annual Christmas lunch. She didn't think she could act happy and carefree. Everyone would be coming back in an upbeat mood because they always used this lunch as an excuse to start celebrating early.

She leaned her head on her desk, tired after so little sleep three nights in a row. At least two of those nights had been worth it, though. She heard footsteps and looked up. Inwardly she groaned.

'Miss Longvale, can I help you?'

Claudia Longvale glared at her. 'We need to have a chat. Looks like poor

Chase is too tenderhearted to tell you the truth.' She pulled off her gloves — supple black leather ones this time, monogrammed with gold on the cuffs.

'The truth? What . . . what do you mean?'

'See, dear, it's like this. I need Chase to do me a favor. It's a simple thing — just pose as my fiancé for a while — but he won't do it because of you.' She tossed her gloves on top of the pile of papers on Darcy's desk.

'I don't know what he sees in you,' Claudia sniffed, 'but that's beside the point.'

Stung, Darcy retorted, 'What are you talking about? Why would you want him to pretend to be your fiancé?'

'That's my business. I want him to, and I always get what I want.'

Darcy bristled. 'Well, maybe not this time.'

'Oh, yes, dear. This time is no exception because if Chase won't do me this little favor then he won't get the financing he needs for Pinto Flats.'

'You're certifiable!' Darcy exclaimed. 'You'd wreck a man's business — his livelihood — because he won't bend to your will?'

'You'd better believe it.'

'Why tell me? What have I got to do with it?'

'You're the reason he won't pretend to be my fiancé. If you step out of the picture, he'll come to his senses.'

Darcy shook her head, sure she was hallucinating the whole ugly incident.

'Do you know what Sunbelt Oil means to Chase Whitaker?' Claudia asked.

The color drained from Darcy's face. Sunbelt was everything to Chase. He'd built the company from the ground up. He'd worked night and day to save it from bankruptcy. Now, just when he thought he'd won, to have it all snatched away! Darcy couldn't stand thinking about it.

'So whether he keeps his company is entirely up to you, Miss Benton.'

Darcy raised anguished eyes. 'Get out

of here,' she said in a low voice.

'I beg your pardon?'

'I said get out while you can do it under your own steam, you pathetic little rich — !' Words failed Darcy. She couldn't think of anything bad enough to call the woman. 'I don't want to ever see you again,' she added.

'I'll go. But remember what I've said. After this party tonight, you'd better be the one to disappear.' She whirled and stalked out of the room, leaving Darcy feeling as if someone had sucked all the life out of her.

Darcy had little doubt that Claudia would do what she'd said. She had to give Chase up or see him ruined. She loved him too much. She couldn't stand the thought of his losing everything because of her.

With greater strength than she thought she possessed, Darcy made her decision. This would be their last night together. Somehow, she'd have to convince him that she wasn't interested in him anymore.

★ ★ ★

Inside the hotel on the River Walk, Darcy barely noticed the thousands of tiny Christmas lights that adorned the lobby and the hall leading to the Fiesta Ballroom. Even the elegant dress she wore brought her no pleasure, nor did the effusive compliments Chase had heaped on her.

She clutched her handbag, feeling as if a grenade were inside it. In a way, the letter she'd written and placed in there was a bomb, just waiting to explode. She'd told him that she couldn't make the commitment to just one man. She'd taken Janet's lie and embroidered it into a picture of a woman unable to control her sensual appetite. If she didn't feel so sad, she'd have laughed at what she'd written.

Chase looked exhausted. He had never made it to the office, but he had called in midafternoon to explain why he had stood her up. He'd spent all of yesterday afternoon and the evening in consultation with Claudia's father. In fact, that was where he had called her from.

Apparently, Claudia was already making waves.

'What's the matter, Darcy?' he asked, stopping and turning to look closely at her.

Darcy knew she had to begin her act. And it had to convince him.

She forced a laugh. 'Nothing is wrong. Come on,' she tugged on his arm. 'I'm ready to party.' Kamikaze butterflies dive-bombed in her stomach. She realized that she hadn't had anything to eat all day. That didn't bode well for the evening she had planned.

'Then party it is,' he said.

There were about a hundred people in the ballroom when they entered. The band was playing and a few couples danced. Darcy shivered. It was going to be a long night.

She cruised the room on Chase's arm, looking for a likely candidate. When she saw Janet talking to a handsome, dark-haired man, she decided he would do as well as the next.

'Chase, there's Janet. Who's the gorgeous hunk standing next to her?'

Chase frowned. 'If you mean that man, that's Victor Santos. He's chief legal counsel for Jack Longvale, Claudia's father.'

That was even better, Darcy thought. 'Come on. You can introduce us.'

Chase trailed her as she rushed over to Janet. When Chase introduced Darcy to Victor, Darcy stared into Victor's eyes and forced herself to hold his hand just a fraction too long. She saw how this displeased Chase. Her confidence that this was the way to scare Chase off slipped a notch. But she couldn't think of anything else to do.

So she flirted. She just hoped she was doing it right. Catching a glance at the anger smoldering in Chase's eyes, she figured she must be.

'Darcy, are you feeling all right tonight?' Janet asked, looking puzzled.

'I feel fine, Janet. I could use a drink,

240

though, I think.'

She turned to Chase. 'Mr. Whitaker, would you get me some of that lovely champagne while I stay here and chat with Victor?'

His brows rose. 'Mr. Whitaker?' Chase looked as if he wanted to refuse, but he said, 'Sure.'

'In fact, I'll help,' Janet said.

'Why?' Darcy asked, staring at her friend and willing her to keep her mouth shut. She grabbed Janet and whispered urgently, 'Stay out of this.'

Janet scowled at her. 'I learned my lesson, thank you.' She took Chase's arm. 'Come on, pal. Walk me back to my date. The company here is too weird.'

Darcy batted her eyes at Victor and wondered if that looked as ridiculous as it felt.

Darcy fell silent as soon as Chase walked away with Janet. Well, she'd done it. Surely, after reading her letter, he'd be convinced.

'Do you have something in your eye, Darcy?' Victor Santos asked.

Embarrassed, Darcy shook her head.

'Then why don't we dance?' He held out his arms to her. Reluctantly, she nodded. She felt Chase's eyes on her from across the room. They swayed to one of the poignant Christmas songs from the rock era. She saw Chase and Janet talking heatedly. She forced herself to smile at Victor.

'If you're in love with Whitaker, why are you throwing yourself at me?' Santos asked.

Darcy grimaced. 'Is it that obvious?'

He smiled. 'Maybe only to me. I'm not used to beautiful women using me to make another man jealous.'

'That's not exactly what I'm trying to do. I'm sorry. You're a very nice man.' They danced without saying anything for a minute. She felt him stiffen, and followed his line of sight.

'Do you know Claudia Longvale?' she asked, curious at his reaction to the woman who'd just entered with her father.

'Yes.' His voice didn't invite further

questions, but his eyes smoldered when he looked at the woman. 'She likes to play games, too. When you've been subjected to a few of these female tricks, you get to where you can recognize them more easily.'

The music ended. They strolled over to where Chase and Janet stood. Chase eyed them speculatively.

Santos winked at Darcy so only she could see. 'Darcy, I'll call you next week,' he said.

'I think that's enough party for now,' Chase said. 'Enjoy the evening, everyone. Please excuse us.'

Darcy's heart hammered as he led her to the lobby. 'Are we leaving?' Surely he'd take her home now. Then she'd give him her farewell letter. And it would be over. He could get back to his life. He'd have his company — safe and sound. And she'd make a new life for herself. Alone.

'Not exactly,' he said, bypassing the exit doors and heading to the bank of elevators.

'Oh!' Darcy said softly.

'Oh, indeed,' Chase replied, winking.

'Good. We have some things to talk about.'

'Sure,' Chase said with a grin. 'We can do that too. Later.'

17

Darcy lay quietly in Chase's arms and waited for him to fall asleep. Then she opened her eyes and watched him, memorizing his features, the texture of his hair, the smell of his skin.

These brief moments would have to last forever. She wouldn't be able to work for Sunbelt Oil after this. Funny, Bruce had been right but for the wrong reasons.

Though Chase had never said he loved her, she knew he cared for her and that this would hurt. But he'd get over her. After all, this was just an affair.

When she was certain that he slept soundly, she pressed one last kiss to his mouth and got dressed. She placed the letter she'd written next to the telephone where he couldn't miss it.

Then, she resolutely walked out of

his life. The elevator whisked her to the lobby. It was past twelve. The party was definitely over, and even the hardiest souls had called it a night.

Her mind was blessedly numb as she rode in the cab home. There, she called Bruce. The ominous silence from him when she told him she planned to spend Christmas at their parents' beach house in Galveston made her realize that he wasn't going to go along easily.

When Bruce arrived, Darcy replied calmly when he roared, 'Did he dump you?'

'No, and keep your voice down. I just decided that the best thing to do is bow out of the picture. When I get back from Galveston, I'll look for another job.'

Relentlessly, Bruce questioned her. Battered by his endless probing, Darcy finally told him everything.

'I don't think you should do this, Stretch.' Grudgingly, he added, 'Whitaker seems like a straight shooter. He can take the heat.'

'But he'd lose everything that's

important to him, Bruce. I love him too much to let that happen.'

'Maybe that's not your decision to make,' he said.

'I have to be strong enough to make it,' Darcy said, determined.

Bruce snorted. 'Sometimes I think most of the problems in the world are created by love. Isn't there anything I can do to change your mind?'

'Not a thing,' Darcy answered. 'I have to do this. One of these days you'll fall in love and you'll do whatever is necessary to protect the one you love. Then you'll understand.'

He grunted, 'Not likely.'

Darcy allowed herself a small smile. Bruce was too handsome to escape Cupid's arrow forever. It was just a matter of time.

'Does Whitaker even know you're leaving town?'

'No. And you better not tell him either.' She finally got Bruce to promise he wouldn't. He carried her bag downstairs.

'How long are you going to be at the beach house?' he asked, raking her with his silver eyes, his expression inscrutable.

'A few days.'

'But what about Christmas? You can't be alone on Christmas.'

'I was going to be anyway since you were working,' she reminded him with a brave smile.

'Well, I would have managed to swing by and spend a little time with you,' he said diffidently.

* * *

Chase knew that he should have talked first and loved second last night. But Darcy had looked so beautiful — so incredibly sexy — that he hadn't been able to wait. But he hadn't expected her to behave so impetuously.

Some day, they'd both laugh at the letter, near comical in light of what he knew, that she'd left for him. As upset as he was at her having left his side during the night, he'd still smiled as he'd read it.

Now he was paying for his impatience, he thought, walking into his office. He flipped on lights and headed for Darcy's cubicle, thinking, hoping that he'd find her there, but she wasn't there.

He saw the black leather gloves lying on Darcy's desk. They weren't hers. His thumb rubbed over the gold monogram. The final piece of the puzzle fell into place.

All he had to do now was find the woman he loved.

★   ★   ★

Resolutely, Darcy drove, refusing to give in to her emotions. She counted the many creeks she crossed, beginning with Woman Hollering creek at the edge of San Antonio, saying the picturesque names aloud, just as she had when she'd been a kid and they'd made the drive to the beach house.

The five hour drive to Galveston took longer than usual since holiday traffic clogged the interstate. By the time Darcy pulled onto the ferry boat in Galveston to go across to Crystal Beach on Bolivar Peninsular, she had to fight to keep her eyes open even though it was just past midday.

Finally, she pulled into the driveway and parked under the house, which was built on twelve foot pilings. The temperature had begun to drop and the wind picked up. The rest of the houses seemed to be shuttered. She was probably alone, she decided dully.

She hauled her suitcase up the stairs and unlocked the house. Opening the windows to let the Gulf breeze blow out the musty, damp smell, she shivered and walked to the bedroom which she usually used. She dropped her suitcase on the floor next to the bed. What was Chase doing now? Would he hate her after he read her letter? She hoped not. He'd probably just chalk it up to experience as a failed affair and let it go at that. She might be a hopeless romantic, but he was a man of the world.

Listlessly, she sat on the bed and wondered what to do now. It had seemed important to get away from Chase, away from San Antonio, but now that she was here, she didn't know why she had come.

After a while, she began to shiver. She went around and closed all the windows she'd opened, then turned the central heat thermostat up. It was going to be cold tonight.

Her stomach growled loudly. 'Well, I guess life goes on,' she said aloud, 'even when you think your heart is broken.'

★   ★   ★

Chase grabbed the phone on the first ring. 'Benton?'

To his relief, it was Darcy's brother. He'd called every Bruce Benton in the phone book, leaving messages on all the answering machines.

251

'Meet me at the diner across the street from the downtown station,' Bruce said.

Chase wasted no time getting there. It was already dark. Darcy had been gone since last night.

Bruce was seated at a booth when he walked in.

Chase withstood the cop's scrutiny until their orders came. Then as he watched Bruce put away an all-you-can-eat breakfast, he told Darcy's brother everything, or nearly everything, before asking, 'Do you know where she is?'

'Yep. I promised her not to call and tell you, but seeing as how you came to me, I guess I'm not breaking any promises.' Eyes twinkling, he continued, 'You may have a hard time convincing her to come back. She's decided to save you from yourself.'

'Where is she?' Chase asked, rubbing his gritty eyes.

'She's at Crystal Beach in Galveston at our family's vacation house. I'll draw you a map. Hell! I'll even give you my key.' He pulled out his key ring and slid one off, handing it to Chase who pocketed it and the map that Bruce drew on a napkin.

'Good luck, Whitaker. You'll need it. Nobody is more stubborn than my sister when she thinks she's doing what's good for somebody she loves.'

Chase grinned and walked out to his Cadillac. He made only one stop, at a novelty shop to pick up some suspenders reminiscent of the elderly man they'd met that first night in the supermarket.

By the time he arrived in Galveston, the ferries to Bolivar Peninsular had stopped running so he had to backtrack and take the long way.

When he finally parked his Cadillac next to Darcy's car beneath the beach house, he felt like a zombie. He decided to close his eyes and rest a bit. Then he'd be refreshed enough to make it up the stairs and fall into her arms. Within minutes he was sound asleep.

Gray light peeked through the curtains, rousing Darcy. She groaned and pulled a pillow over her head. She wanted desperately to go back to sleep, but it was no use. The world came crashing in on her as she lay there, longing for the one person in the world who made her complete.

She needed coffee, Darcy decided, stepping into her slippers. She nudged the thermostat up on her way to the kitchen, glad she'd brought her old flannel pajamas to wear.

While the coffee brewed, she opened the drapes. The morning looked wet and gray — as gray as she felt. Remnants of fog floated above the ground. She saw a pile of newspapers in one of the neighbor's yards and decided to raid it. They obviously weren't at home so they wouldn't miss it. And she needed something to occupy her thoughts.

Carrying a mug full of black coffee,

she started down the stairs. She nearly tumbled down the steps when she saw the pearl-white Cadillac parked next to her car. She must be hallucinating, she thought, going up to it. When she tapped on the window, Chase stirred. He shifted on the seat but didn't open his eyes. He was no figment of her imagination, even if he was wearing candy-cane striped suspenders.

Darcy opened the car door. His eyes opened at the same time. He smiled at her and reached for her coffee cup as if she'd come to wake him with the fragrant brew.

'What are you doing here?' Darcy asked, not knowing whether to give in to surprise or anger or joy. Her heart beat fast and then faster. She closed her eyes and opened them, but he was still there.

'How did you get here?'

'I drove.'

Darcy shook her head. 'But why?'

'So we could spend Christmas together.' He leaned close and kissed her sweetly on the lips. 'Merry Christmas, darling.'

Darcy fought his sweet words. 'No. You can't. I mean, this is crazy. You're supposed to be in San Antonio.'

'No, I'm supposed to be with you.' He kissed her cheek. 'Today and every Christmas until we both croak.'

'How romantic. Chase, this won't work.' She had to make him go back. She couldn't be responsible for him losing Sunbelt Oil.

'Sure it will.'

'No, it won't. I don't want you anymore,' Darcy said, desperate to convince him to leave.

'You don't?' he asked. He didn't seem perturbed by her rejection.

'No. I want other men,' she said desperately, 'lots of other men. Didn't you read my letter?'

He grinned. 'Every word. Maybe I could wear a wig or a fake beard and you can pretend I'm a different man. I could get a wardrobe of disguises if you like.'

'Chase, do I have to spell it out?

Didn't Janet tell you what a . . . a playgirl I am? Love 'em and leave 'em. That's my motto. It would be boring to sleep with the same man, night after night.' Her heart hammered. Why wasn't he getting angry?

'Well, I guess I'll just have to try my best to keep it exciting,' he said, grasping the lapels of her pajama shirt. 'Maybe you could give me pointers from your vast experience,' he said, sliding over on the car seat and pulling Darcy with him. She was so intent on convincing him to leave that she didn't resist.

'Chase, you don't want me. I lied when I said I was a playgirl. I'm just a plain, ordinary, dull . . . accountant!'

'I know,' he said.

'You deserve someone like,' Darcy nearly gagged, 'like Claudia Longvale.'

'Nope. I want you.'

'But why? Why would you want me?'

'For a million reasons. Because you're smart, and beautiful. Because I find it incredibly charming that you think you need to save me.' He grinned crookedly. 'No one has ever tried to save me before. It's quite a humbling experience to realize you'd give up everything important to you just to protect me. And last of all, because I love you.'

His smile and his tender words stole her breath away.

'Darcy, I know all about Janet's trick — and about Claudia's chat with you. She's not going to cause problems. Her father will see to that. If I'm right, Victor Santos will help her dad with the problem.'

He stroked her face. 'How could you even think I'd let you go? Regardless of what was at stake? Even if Claudia followed through with her threat, there are more important things in life than Sunbelt Oil. I can live without my company, but I'm not certain I can live without you.'

When he reached for the buttons on his shirt, she asked, 'What are you doing?'

'I'm giving you your Christmas present.'

The intensity burning in his gorgeous blue eyes mesmerized Darcy. 'What is it?' she asked.

'Me.'

Epilogue

Christmas — One Year Later

Chase whistled appreciatively as Darcy twirled in front of the mirror. He walked up behind her, encircling her body with his arms, and nuzzled her neck.

'Umm, you smell nice,' he murmured, kissing her bare shoulder. His hand reached down to slide up her leg and beneath the hem of the emerald green dress. 'Isn't this dress a little short?' he complained.

'You always say that.' Darcy laughingly ignored his question.

Anticipation raced up her nerve endings. 'Do you think we'll manage to stay longer at the party this year?' she teased, watching Chase in the mirror. How handsome her husband was!

'I don't know. You're awfully tempting.' His palm slid along the ivory skin revealed by the strapless velvet dress. She sighed as he traced the neckline of the dress and down the length of her slender arms.

'Are you sure you wouldn't like to wear a nice boxy business suit with a simple white blouse and a bow tie?'

'Quite sure,' Darcy replied with a grin.

'It would be a lot more comfortable than this tight dress.' His hands stroked over her hips, following her familiar curves.

Darcy could barely think. It had been a year and she never tired of his touch.

'You know I gave all those suits to the Salvation Army,' she said. Her eyes twinkled. Never had she imagined such perfection could be had in life.

Darcy placed her hands over Chase's and guided them until they lay on her flat stomach. She watched his reflection so she could see his reaction to her next words.

'I wanted to wear this for you so you'd be able to remember, in a few months, what I look like under normal circumstances.'

His breath seemed to catch in his throat. His eyes jerked to meet hers in the mirror.

'What are you trying to tell me?' Chase whispered.

'Merry Christmas, darling.' Darcy's smile was tender and filled with love for him. Tears of happiness, sparkling brighter than the diamonds on her wedding ring, made her gray eyes shine. 'I hope our baby has your beautiful blue eyes.'

We do hope that you have enjoyed reading this large print book.

Did you know that all of our titles are available for purchase?

We publish a wide range of high quality large print books including:
Romances, Mysteries, Classics
General Fiction
Non Fiction and Westerns

Special interest titles available in large print are:
The Little Oxford Dictionary
Music Book, Song Book
Hymn Book, Service Book

Also available from us courtesy of Oxford University Press:
Young Readers' Dictionary
(large print edition)
Young Readers' Thesaurus
(large print edition)

For further information or a free brochure, please contact us at:
Ulverscroft Large Print Books Ltd.,
The Green, Bradgate Road, Anstey,
Leicester, LE7 7FU, England.
Tel: (00 44) **0116 236 4325**
Fax: (00 44) **0116 234 0205**

TWISTED TAPESTRIES

Joyce Johnson

Jenna Pascoe is a Cornish fisherman's daughter. When her parents receive news that her mother's sister, aunt Olive, is coming home to England from Italy, they refuse to acknowledge her. Family secrets resurface and Jenna's initial delight turns to dismay. However, Olive and her family turn up at their home, and Jenna meets her handsome cousin Allesandro. How will the families resolve their differences — and how will cousins, Jenna and Allesandro cope with their growing feelings for each other . . . ?